HITOPADESHA

Also by Shonaleeka Kaul

'Looking Within': Life Lessons from Lal Ded

Cultural History of Early South Asia

*The Making of Early Kashmir:
Landscape and Identity in the Rajatarangini*

*Eloquent Spaces: Meaning and Community
in Early Indian Architecture*

Imagining the Urban: Sanskrit and the City in Early India

*Retelling Time: Alternative Temporalities
from Premodern South Asia*

HITOPADESHA
BY NARAYANA

A NEW ENGLISH TRANSLATION

SHONALEEKA KAUL

Illustrated by Krishna Bala Shenoi

ALEPH

ALEPH BOOK COMPANY
An independent publishing firm
promoted by *Rupa Publications India*

First published in India in 2022
by Aleph Book Company
7/16 Ansari Road, Daryaganj
New Delhi 110 002

Copyright © Shonaleeka Kaul 2022

The translator has asserted her moral rights.

All rights reserved.

This is a work of fiction. Names, characters,
places, and incidents are either the product of the
author's imagination or are used fictitiously and any
resemblance to any actual persons, living or dead,
events, or locales is entirely coincidental.

No part of this publication may be reproduced,
transmitted, or stored in a retrieval system, in any
form or by any means, without permission in writing
from Aleph Book Company.

ISBN: 978-93-91047-94-8

3 5 7 9 10 8 6 4

Printed in India

This book is sold subject to the condition that it
shall not, by way of trade or otherwise, be lent,
resold, hired out, or otherwise circulated without the
publisher's prior consent in any form of binding or
cover other than that in which it is published.

śrīkṛṣṇārpaṇamastu

In loving memory of
Buzky

(2006–2020)
A Lion of a Dog

CONTENTS

Introduction / ix

Prologue: How It All Began / 1

Book One: Winning Friends / 11

Book Two: Losing Friends / 67

Book Three: Waging War / 119

Book Four: Making Peace / 161

Acknowledgements / 199

INTRODUCTION

'Hitopadesha' literally means 'good advice'. The ancient Sanskrit text of that name, which is translated here into English for modern readers, is an epigrammatic text in mixed prose and verse that brings together good advice, drawing on a popular theme or genre of thought and literature in early India known as niti. Niti is usually translated as 'principles of polity and/or morality'. But, as readers will see, niti as represented in a collection of stories like the *Hitopadesha* went well beyond the political and the moral to embrace the simply practical. Prescribing canny and pragmatic responses to a range of very human situations, ambitions, problems, and dilemmas, niti, as invoked repeatedly in the *Hitopadesha*, is really the knowledge and art of prudent conduct. And the text disseminates this knowledge in the form of illustrative stories, fables, and maxims involving the lives of humans and animals.

The *Hitopadesha* was probably composed in the ninth or tenth century CE, and scholars conjecture that it may have been produced in some part of eastern India where a number (though not all) of its manuscripts were discovered in the nineteenth century. As the colophons of the text tell us, it was composed by a scholar called Pandit Narayana and sponsored and promoted by a medieval Indian ruler called Dhavalachandra, whose role the poet acknowledges briefly at the end of his composition. Beyond this, however, as is common for much of Sanskrit literature, we do not know anything about the author and his context.

Initially, in fact, before the particular manuscript carrying Narayana's name was found, it was not known that any such person was the composer of this work. The *Hitopadesha* was credited instead by scholars and early translators to Vishnusharma, the sage who figures in the text and narrates all its stories. Vishnusharma is also known to be the composer of that other world-famous Sanskrit fable, the *Panchatantra*, and since there was a great deal in common between the *Hitopadesha* and the *Panchatantra*, it was assumed that they had one and the same authorship. Now we know that is not the case.

◆

However, the question of the authorship of the *Hitopadesha* remains complicated because of the nature of the text. Rather than an original work from start to finish, it is for the most part an anthology or collection of verses, perspectives, and teachings from a host of other seminal Sanskrit texts of the Indic civilization.

Anthologizing in this manner was not unheard of in early India and other examples of texts have come down to us that preserve what were obviously considered in their time important as well as elegantly turned verses—or entire stories—from multiple compositions across ages. These include the *Subhashitaratnakosha* in Sanskrit (eleventh century CE) and the much earlier *Gathasaptashati* in Prakrit (second century CE). In fact, the *Hitopadesha* itself came to be excerpted in later texts in like fashion.

Another way to understand this is that multiple texts drew on a common reservoir of free-floating iconic tales. Beyond explicit and verbatim borrowings, the phenomenon of intertextual awareness—texts referencing or echoing other texts—was a noticeable feature of Sanskrit literary culture as a whole. It points to the well-knit circulatory sphere of aesthetics and the composite thought-world these texts inhabited and were constantly dialoguing with. It may also suggest the overarching ethos and ideals that most, if not all, such works in early India upheld even as they had their own unique things to add.

The *Hitopadesha* accordingly includes verses and voices from the two epics, the Ramayana and Mahabharata, most notably the Bhagavad Gita from the latter work; texts on diplomacy and statecraft like Kamandaka's *Nitisara*; socio-legal treatises called the *Dharmashastras*; a compendium on niti by Bhartrihari called the *Nitishataka*; and of course the fables of the *Panchatantra*, which is said to be the source of about three-quarters of the *Hitopadesha*'s content. The *Hitopadesha* itself admits its debt to the *Panchatantra*.

In fact, the frame story of the two texts is identical in so far as the narration of both the *Hitopadesha* and the *Panchatantra* is occasioned by a king's need to educate his lazy and worthless sons in statesmanship and in worldly wisdom more generally. The way this proceeds is also the same in the two compositions, namely, a pandit, Vishnusharma, an expert in nitishastra, is assigned the job, and he chooses to bring home to the uninitiated princes the subtle teachings of prudent conduct through a large number of tales, each one emerging from the one before it. A palimpsest of stories—a frame story with multiple sub-stories which have autonomous, stand-alone plots but loop back to the original from time to time—is, again, a common narrative technique in the world of Sanskrit literature. Bana's *Kadambari* (seventh century CE) and the Mahabharata itself are excellent examples of such metanarratives.

The *Hitopadesha* tales include, for the most part, anthropomorphized birds and animals who speak and are imbued with all too human qualities and frailties; they also serve as narrators for many of the sub-stories. Some tales, however, feature only humans while others have men, women, and animals play their parts. The stories revolving around these characters are arranged in four fascinating books or sections: Winning Friends, Losing Friends, Waging War, and Making Peace. The *Panchatantra* sports these same sections and an additional fifth one (actually the fourth in that text, which the *Hitopadesha* does away with).

Now, despite the fact that the *Hitopadesha* brings together perspectives and maxims from a range of other influential Indic texts, it should not be assumed that these verses are haphazardly thrown together to come up with an unoriginal and incoherent work! The *Hitopadesha* does possess at least three dozen new stories of its own, and also reads very cogently and logically, as stories flow in and out of each other and always serve the larger purpose and intent of the text and its narrator, which is to lay out and illustrate in easy, palatable, and digestible form principles of political wisdom and pragmatic living. It has advice for not only the ruler who is too timid or too haughty to know what is good for him and his subjects, but for the minister or follower who must serve him, as also for the innocent husband with the conniving wife, the beautiful wife with the undeserving husband, owners of pets who don't understand their loyalty, greedy people, distraught people, friends turned enemies, enemies reconciled, clever people, foolish people, and so on.

◆

In its more recent career, the *Hitopadesha*, again like the *Panchatantra*, is among the most widely translated classical texts from India. It was in fact only the second text selected by the British to be rendered into English in 1787 by Charles

Wilkins, who had in 1784 brought out no less a work than the Bhagavad Gita in like fashion. Several more editions and English translations followed till as recently as 2007, the one by the veteran Sanskrit scholar M. R. Kale in 1896 with multiple reprints perhaps being the best known of the lot.

The *Hitopadesha* has also appeared in a large number of Indian regional languages including Hindi, Bengali, Gujarati, Kannada, Malayalam, Tamil, Telugu, Marathi, and Odia. Moreover, it has been translated into a little more than a dozen foreign languages, including French, German, Dutch, Greek, Russian, Spanish, Newari, Thai, Malay, Persian, and Sinhala.

What explains the immense popularity of this work within and well beyond its originary culture? One reason would no doubt be the playful, fablesque form of the tales and lessons the *Hitopadesha* narrates. Fables and folklore have always had a wide cross-cultural provenance and appeal. Further, it is precisely this flexibility to adopt an aesthetic and appealing mode that distinguished Sanskrit literature (kavya) from the rather more sedate requirements of a treatise (shastra). And a down-to-earth rather than exalted mode of representation would naturally have won a wider audience in the text's own time, just as today.

However, it may also be the case that the high emotional quotient of the text—the range of human emotions and situations the *Hitopadesha* presents, and the clever solutions and 'behaviour management techniques' it proposes to ensure sheer survival and success in a difficult world—has a decidedly universal resonance. A guide to surviving life and relationships speaks, perhaps, to the basic psychological needs of most people in societies across the globe. So, even though the imagery, locales, and metaphors in the *Hitopadesha* are all very much Indic, its appeal transcends the limits of geography.

Indeed, the overt lightness and childlike quality of the

literary treatment found in the *Hitopadesha*—the use of animals as protagonists, humour, satire, pranks, unconventional thought and behaviour, wild desires, and foolish deeds etc.—should not make us lose sight of the fundamental didacticism of literature of this kind. Moreover, as we will see, its socio-emotional pedagogy as well as, one dare say, its unorthodox and irreverent take on human behaviour, are also what give the *Hitopadesha* an evergreen flavour—a continuing relevance well into our modern lives. This is contrary to the fairly widespread misconception today that Sanskrit literature is archaic and far removed from modern sensibilities or contexts.

◆

Some special aspects of the text further elucidate the lively and provocative nature of the *Hitopadesha*, but are rarely discussed in existing translations and studies as anything more than instances of tongue-in-cheek humour. One such remarkable aspect is that, again unlike all expectations and stereotypes today about Sanskrit literature, which is rather sweepingly regarded as conservative and geared towards reproducing social hierarchies, a didactic work like the *Hitopadesha* could simultaneously be antinomic.

In other words, it could and did critique and lampoon figures of power and social ideals. Thus, even in a story commissioned by and addressed to royalty, the king is routinely shown as unwise, clueless, haughty, dependent, or gullible. In fact the last two books of the *Hitopadesha* are entirely about a couple of impetuous kings, albeit of the feathered variety, and the easily provoked, needless war between them. It is only through the wise counsel and strategies of their respective ministers, also birds, that peace is ultimately secured. The satire on kings as rather risky liabilities is a constant in these tales.

Then, the figure of the Brahmin, who stands at the head of the socio-ritual caste hierarchy and represents learning and scriptures, is also satirized in, for example, the parodical story of the old tiger, which we shall discuss further below. Given that both the author and narrator of our text are Brahmin, a sagacious capacity for self-critique appears in relief here. However, perhaps the most sensational example of the text's unorthodoxy is the fact that women are occasionally shown indulging in extramarital affairs in the *Hitopadesha*. They are also represented, with the text's light touch always, as libidinous and resourceful characters who go after what they want despite social sanctions. This may be read as misogyny by some but may also reflect considerable female agency in early India, something that is visible in other works of Sanskrit poetry and prose as well. Sample some of these textual comments:

> Women have twice the appetite of men
> four times their brains
> six times their courage
> and eight times their libido! (2.7.119)

> Neither modesty, nor decorum,
> good sense nor fear
> keep women chaste.
> It is only the absence of a suitor that does! (1.6.119)

Now, these provocative lines need not be read as relating to a licentious society, far from it, as we will see below. Reflecting layered social critique, the text instead displays—not without some sympathy—the complexity of male and female psyches. In the process, if didactic literature in early India could shape ethical subjectivity, it could confound it as well. For this reason I propose a new descriptor for the *Hitopadesha* and allied texts:

the antinomic didactic. Consider, for example, the story of a young and sensuous woman who is forced into marriage with an old and lustful merchant. He is shown as not being able to satisfy her, driving her to take a young and vigorous lover. In this context, the text rather unabashedly declares:

> Women have no interest in husbands
> with old and weathered organs.
> Aged men are hardly virile.
> Their wives are taken with other men
> and regard the husband
> as a necessary evil, just like medicine! (1.6.109–10)

But:

> While living beings lust for life and wealth,
> the aged man desires a young wife more than life itself!
> An old man can neither enjoy sense-pleasures
> nor renounce them.
> He is like an old, toothless dog
> who cannot chew the bone
> but helplessly licks at it. (1.6.111–12)

The *Hitopadesha* is thus remarkably observant and candid about behavioural and relationship paradoxes. It is, further, rather unsentimental about social ideals and perhaps inclines towards representing social reality more, which is always complicated. Thus, again, we have the deeply satirical tale about a wicked tiger who, having ostentatiously bathed himself and holding sacred grass in his hand, pretends to be pious and righteous in order to ensnare unsuspecting passers-by as prey. He addresses a traveller he is trying to lure thus:

> I was a bad sort in my youth. I killed a number of men and cows…. Then a holy man advised me to cultivate

dharma and perform charity. It is thanks to his advice that
I am now a pious and generous old tiger.... Can I not be
trusted then?

...But who cares? It will still be said that tigers only eat men!
Because:

> Fixed in their old ways, the world will not believe a
> prostitute
> who may speak about dharma
> but will only believe a Brahmin on the subject
> even if he be a sinner. (1.2.8–10)

After spouting this disingenuous yet insightful comment on the ways of the world, the tiger of course went on to trap and kill the foolish traveller, whose last thoughts were:

> How does reading the sacred books
> emancipate a villain?
> Nature and temperament alone are supreme
> in shaping a person. (1.2.17)

Socio-religious satire is thus underwritten here by an important practical observation about life. Its purpose, then, is not to merely mock this class or that, since elsewhere in the text Brahmins are praised as innocent and trustworthy, kings are shown as personally invested in justice, and women as bearers of a deep common sense. The point of the antinomy lay elsewhere: to contrast the ideal with the real and the sacred with the profane, since the world where people must act was both real and profane. The moral of the story? In the words of the *Hitopadesha:*

> Therefore, one must never act without thinking things
> through. Because:

> Well-thought words and well-considered actions
> like well-digested food, a well-educated child,
> a well-taught wife and a well-served king
> never give bad results. (1.2.22)

Indeed, if anything, the *Hitopadesha* comes across as highly realist literature and as such may be understood as a complement to the idealism of the Shastras. Gnomic literature teaches us how to survive with ideals in a less than ideal world.

In fact, we may go so far as to say that the *Hitopadesha* appears as something of a survival guide for the innocent, the good, and the weak—a constituency the text invokes often, both directly and through its characters—and attempts to educate them on how to make it in an unfair and devious world, using nothing but the power of superior intellect. As the text says:

> Just because you have done someone no harm
> is no reason to trust that they will not harm you either.
> Good people have always reason to fear the bad
> who do not care for virtue and vice. (2.4.75)

> A crook speaking sweetly is no reason to trust him.
> He will have honey on his lips
> but deadly poison fills his heart. (2.4.81)

But, no matter how much more powerful the villainous enemy, the *Hitopadesha*'s ringing call is the famous quote 'matireva balad gariyasi', or 'brains are mightier than brawn' (2.4.86/87), also phrased as 'upayen hi yacchakyam na tacchakyam parakramaih', or 'that which is possible by stratagem is not possible even by valour' (1.9.202, 2.7.120). This, in a sense, sums up the whole text since niti is all about training and applying the mind to overcome all manner of adversaries and adversities.

Having said that, the ever pragmatic *Hitopadesha* is nuanced enough to also make the point elsewhere that it is unwise to confront an enemy who is much more powerful than oneself, for loss is a certainty in such a battle. This may appear a bit of a contradiction on the part of the text—one of several that can be spotted when the *Hitopadesha* is read closely.

For example, while the text laments poverty and exhorts industry and labour to gain wealth, it also decries great wealth or an obsession with it. And even though it undermines wealth in this way, many verses are devoted to what can only be described as consumerism. Thus the text repeatedly emphasizes spending wealth on acquiring all the pleasures of life as opposed to hoarding riches.

Similarly, while the renunciation of worldly desires is espoused at one point along with contentment with what little one possesses, it is precisely contentment with one's lot that is indicted at another place for obstructing growth and expansion. And then again, the philosophy or world view of the *Hitopadesha* appears to oscillate between a powerful fatalism and the corresponding helplessness of humans before inscrutable destiny on the one hand, and the strength of human resolve and effort to shape their own outcome on the other.

How should we understand these apparent contradictions and inconsistencies? Perhaps these reflect an attempt to help readers reconcile to the realities of life and its unpredictable nature while keeping them going against all odds at the same time. Perhaps on view is also an attempt to balance extremes like asceticism and hedonism, prescribing instead a healthy mean which consists of living life to the fullest, yet not losing oneself while at it. Above all, perhaps, what these changing positions tell is a tale of changing contexts that we will encounter in life, so that discerning action according to the context alone is wisdom (pandityam paricchedah, 2.148).

Another admirable aspect of the *Hitopadesha* is its fine reading of human nature and psychology. As if to make the point explicit, the *Hitopadesha* even includes in Book Two (3.50–52) advice on precisely how to read the inner workings of someone else's mind from their gestures and expressions. Less explicit but no less telling are the following maxims from miscellaneous stories in the *Hitopadesha*. Apart from subtle psychological commentaries, these also contain gems of sociological and political insight, as well as a reflection, yet again, of the *Hitopadesha*'s pragmatism, which is shorn of any standing on prestige when deciding on the best course of action:

> Good people think everyone else is good too.
> And so, they are easily cheated by the wicked. (4.9.52)

> People deceived by the wicked
> cease to trust even the good.
> Like a child burnt by porridge
> blows at even yoghurt to cool it down. (4.13.102)

> Indeed, in the absence of learned people
> even the semi-literate gain a reputation!
> Just as in arid lands where no trees grow,
> even the castor oil palm is considered a tree! (1.4. 69)

> A starving woman forsakes even her son.
> A starving serpent devours its own eggs.
> One hungry will commit any sin.
> The weak person knows no compassion. (4.9.54)

> There are worries enough in this lifetime

than to want to court the sorrow
of not having the possessions you crave.
That craving is without end. (1.7.187)

It is possible that jewels may languish on the feet
while beads of glass adorn the head.
Each, however, stays what it is: a jewel is a jewel
glass is merely glass. (2.3.69)

Every person should be deployed
according to their respective expertise.
Otherwise even an intelligent man
will falter at an unfamiliar task. (3.7.53/54)

When required, a good strategy, great bravery,
heroic fighting, as well as fleeing for one's life
must be resorted to without a moment's thought! (3.140)

A king's policies, especially, must be variegated
like those of a whore:
sometimes honest, sometimes not,
sometimes harsh, sometimes soft,
sometimes violent, sometimes tolerant,
sometimes acquisitive, sometimes generous,
sometimes extravagant, sometimes restrained. (2.182)

Learning does not help one
who is afraid to act.
Just as a lamp held by a blind man
cannot show him the way.' (1.7.171)

As these vignettes convey, the *Hitopadesha* touches on myriad human situations and responses, balancing idealism with pragmatism, and seeking to infuse and align them with niti, or prudence. The goal appears to be welfare and success for the individual as much as for the social or political formation at large. And yet, it operates with a realism and lightness of touch that make life itself more relatable and bearable.

The English translation that follows attempts to capture the prodigious *Hitopadesha* in this dimension. Based on the Chowkhamba Sanskrit Sansthan edition of 1951, it is faithful to the original text without being insistently literal. It is rather an idiomatic translation, in simple narrative prose and free verse that prioritizes ease and flow of reading without allowing the awkwardness, stiffness, and obscurity of form that sometimes must accompany verbatim renditions. The meaning has, nonetheless, always been retained.

PROLOGUE
HOW IT ALL BEGAN

May the endeavours of good people
succeed by the grace of Lord Shiva
whose head is adorned by the crescent moon,
which is formed as if by the foam of the river Ganga. (1)

Once heard, the words of wisdom that follow
bestow eloquence not only in Sanskrit
but in all subjects
as well as in the knowledge of niti, or prudent conduct. (2)

One intelligent should pursue knowledge, just like wealth,
as if he is to live forever
and practise dharma, or righteousness,
as if he will die any minute! (3)

Learning is always the best of all possessions
since it is invaluable
yet can never be stolen or lost. (4)

Just as a river carries a humble speck of dust
to merge with the mighty ocean,
so too learning ensures that a commoner
goes places and acquires great fortune. (5)

Learning brings humility,
humility gives rise to competence,
competence earns wealth,
wealth allows for the performance of good deeds,
which in turn bring happiness. (6)

Learning and martial skills both will win you respect.
But martial prowess will decline as you age.
Learning, on the other hand,
will always serve you well. (7)

Childhood, like a pot of clay, is imprinted forever
with what it is exposed to early.
Hence, in the guise of stories, the knowledge of niti
is hereby imparted to children. (8)

Abstracted from the *Panchatantra*
and other ancient works of niti,
these stories are divided into four kinds: Winning Friends,
Losing Friends, Waging War, and Making Peace. (9)

There once was a city named Pataliputra on the banks of the Ganga. There ruled a king by the name of Sudarshana who was endowed with the best of kingly virtues. He once heard someone reciting the following two verses:

'True knowledge is that
which dispels a hundred doubts
and reveals hidden meanings.
Such knowledge is akin to the eyes of the world
and one who does not possess this knowledge
is akin to the blind. (10)

Youth, abundant wealth, power, thoughtlessness
any one of these is enough

to wreak havoc in life.

When all four occur together, there's hell to pay!' (11)

Hearing this, King Sudarshana was reminded of his own sons who refused to study the scriptures and were up to no good. He thought:

> 'What is the point of a son
> who is neither learned nor righteous?
> What use is a shattered eye except to ache? (12)

> It is better not to have a child or to lose the child at birth
> than to have a fool for a child,
> for the first two conditions give grief only once
> but the fool does so at every step. (13)

Moreover,

> Many are born in this world
> and many die only to be born again.
> Only that birth is worthwhile
> which takes the family forward in life. (14)

> A woman who gives birth to a child
> without any good qualities to recommend him
> is the one who is truly childless,
> not a woman who cannot bear a child. (15)

> Indeed, a child who has no interest in charity or penance,
> valour or learning, and acquiring success
> is as worthless as
> his mother's waste matter. (16)

Further:

> Just one talented child is better
> than a hundred foolish ones.

Much like the solitary moon
that dispels the darkness of the night
when a whole bunch of stars fail to. (17)

Only one who has undergone great penance in a holy place,
a person rare and pure,
is blessed with a child who grows up
obedient, learned, righteous, and wealthy. (18)

For there are only six kinds of joys in this world:
health, wealth, knowledge that brings success,
a beloved wife who is sweet of tongue,
and an obedient son. (19)

What is gained from having many a son
who merely consume resources?
Far better to have the one child
who brings repute to his father. (20)

Just like having a father burdened by debt,
a mother gone astray, or a wife who is excessively beautiful,
having a foolish son is a constant risk
as good as having an enemy. (21)

Knowledge to the lazy is like poison
just as food is to one with severe indigestion!
Or as a young woman is fatal for an old man
and a public assembly is fatal for a fool. (22)

A man of talent is respected
regardless of his obscure origins.
For a bow made of the finest wood
is useless without a string. (23)

Therefore, now, by whatever means possible, I must make my sons talented.

For:

> Food, sleep, fear, and sex
> are common to humans and animals.
> It is dharma alone that sets humans apart,
> and one devoid of dharma is no different than an animal. (24)

Therefore:

> He who lacks the urge for the four goals of human life,
> namely, piety, power, pleasure, and liberation—
> there is no point to his birth in this world. (25)

> Some say that one's age, actions, finances,
> education, and death
> are all already determined
> while we are still in the womb. (26)

> And that what has to happen will happen
> even to the gods, not to mention humans.
> For example, Shiva's naked form and Vishnu's serpent-bed
> were destined to happen. (27)

> And, they further believe that he who lacks talent
> can never acquire it
> and he who is talented can never stop being so.
> Therefore, why worry and fret, they say,
> at what cannot be changed? (28)

This, however, is the lazy person's way of thinking!

> In fact, one must never give up effort
> and merely rely on fate, good or bad.
> Without the effort of pressing oil seeds

even they can't yield oil! (29)

Moreover:

> Industrious people, proud and bold like lions,
> are the ones who go out and attract good fortune.
> It is only cowards who accept the limits
> of what fate brings.
> Therefore, shun all thoughts of fate
> and try your best
> at whatever you do.
> If you then don't succeed,
> it will at least not be your fault! (30)
>
> Just as a chariot cannot run on one wheel,
> destiny too cannot manifest
> without human effort. (31)
>
> In any case, fate is nothing but
> our actions in previous lives.
> So, give up sloth and work hard! (32)
>
> Just as a potter shapes a lump of clay
> as he pleases,
> so too do humans make of their lives
> what they will. (33)
>
> Even if you stumble upon hidden treasure suddenly,
> it is you who will have to make the effort
> to seize it.
> Luck cannot do it on your behalf! (34)
>
> You succeed by effort alone
> and not by wishful thinking.
> A lion must hunt to eat;
> the deer will hardly enter his mouth while he sleeps! (35)

> Parents cultivate good qualities in a child
> by consistent practice.
> Nobody emerges learned from the womb! (36)
>
> In fact, parents who do not teach their child
> have acted like enemies to him.
> Such a child will prove a misfit in any public assembly,
> much like a heron among swans. (37)
>
> Though beautiful, well-off, and high-born,
> one without learning is unimpressive,
> like the flaming kinshuk flower
> that possesses not fragrance. (38)
>
> A well-turned-out person, if a fool,
> has only to start speaking
> to stop being attractive.' (39)

Thinking all the while in this manner, King Sudarshana called a meeting with learned men. To them he said: 'Oh pandits! Please pay heed. Is anyone among you capable of giving a new lease of life to my truant sons by instructing them in wise conduct?

For:

> Just like glass in the company of gold
> may glitter like a jewel,
> so too fools may be transformed
> in the company of the learned. (40)

It has indeed been said:

> If surrounded by inferior people,
> the intellect declines.
> If accompanied by people of the same calibre,
> it stagnates.

But if blessed with the proximity of people superior,
the intellect shines.' (41)

At this point, a great pandit named Vishnusharma, who was adept in the science of niti like Lord Brihaspati himself, spoke thus:

'These princes are well born.
They are capable of imbibing
the precepts of wise conduct.

It is true that efforts applied
to an inherently worthless object
do not succeed,
just as no matter how hard you try,
you cannot teach a heron to speak
like you can a parrot. (42)

But this royal family cannot
produce worthless sons
just like a diamond mine cannot
produce pieces of glass. (43)

Therefore, well within six months, I can teach your sons niti, the precepts of prudent conduct.'

Hearing this, the king spoke again most humbly:

'Even an insect may ascend
the head of a celebrity
by attaching itself to flowers.
And mere stone may ascend to godhood
and be worshipped
if consecrated by the hands of virtuous persons. (44)

Just as mountaintops gleam
through proximity to the sun's rays,

so too do the lowly shine
through the company of good people. (45)

Qualities can be appreciated only among the talented.
Those devoid of good sense may regard them as flaws.
Just as the sweet waters of a river turn salty
when they find themselves in the sea. (46)

For all these reasons, you, oh Pandit, are best suited to instruct my sons in niti, the science of wise conduct.'

With these words, King Sudarshana respectfully handed over his sons to Vishnusharma.

BOOK ONE

Winning Friends

Now, as the princes sat all relaxed on the palace terrace, the Pandit said:

> 'Smart people spend their time
> enjoying literature.
> Fools, on the other hand,
> lose time sleeping or fighting. (1)

Hence, for your entertainment, I narrate this wondrous tale of the crow and the tortoise.'

The princes replied: 'Oh noble one, please do!'

Vishnusharma then said: 'So listen, now I present the art of Winning Friends, which begins with the following verse:

> Like the crow, tortoise, deer, and mouse
> who were fast friends,
> even people who lack in wealth and resources
> but have brains and good friends
> succeed quickly in their endeavours.' (2)

The princes exclaimed: 'How?' Vishnusharma began to narrate.

THE FIRST STORY

There is on the banks of the Godavari River a huge shalmali (silk cotton) tree. Birds from many different places come there to nest at night. Once, when dawn was near and the moon was about to set, a crow named Laghupatnaka (Swift Flyer) awoke and beheld a bird-hunter approach, much like Yamaraj, the lord of death. He immediately thought: 'What an inauspicious sight first thing in the morning! Goodness knows what is to follow.' Worried, he began to follow the hunter.

Because:

> A thousand sorrows and a hundred fears
> befall the fool every day
> but not one who is learned and wise. (3)

And those who are engrossed in worldly pursuits should definitely do as follows:

> Waking up in the morning
> they should consider first thing
> what great fear—sickness, sorrow, or death—
> may befall them that day. (4)

Strewing grains of rice on the forest floor, the hunter then laid a net trap over it and, hiding nearby, sat down to wait. Soon the king of pigeons named Chitragriva (Painted Neck), who was flying by with family, saw the strewn rice. He addressed his fellow pigeons, who hungered for the grain, thus: 'How is rice possible in this deserted forest? Think this through first. I think this is a bad omen, and through our greed we may end up like

> The traveller greedy for gold
> who ran aground in deep slush
> and, rendered an easy target even for an old tiger,
> was killed by it.' (5)

The pigeons asked: 'How come?' So, Chitragriva began to narrate:

THE SECOND STORY

While wandering in the southern jungles, I once came upon an old tiger who, having bathed himself clean and holding sacred kusha grass in his hand, said: 'Oh travellers, here, take this golden bangle!' Hearing this, some greedy travellers thought to themselves: 'What great luck! However, I must not act in a way that harms me since:

> Just as life-giving nectar mixed with poison
> will still kill.
> So too attaining one's heart's desire through a villain
> can never turn out well. (6)

However, it is also true that acquiring wealth always entails risk.

> Which is why it is said:
> Success is never attained without some doubt.
> But one must also remain alive to attain it! (7)

So let me check this out first.' The traveller thus spoke aloud: 'Where is your bangle?' The tiger opened his palm and showed it. The traveller asked again: 'How do I trust a predator like you?' The tiger replied: 'Listen, oh traveller! I was a bad sort in my youth. I killed a number of men and cows. Due to the sin of their deaths, my wife and children also died, leaving me without an heir. Then a holy man advised me to cultivate dharma and perform charity. It is thanks to his advice that I am now a pious and generous old tiger whose teeth and nails, in any case, have dissolved with age. Can I not be trusted then?

For:

> Performing rituals, studying the scriptures,
> philanthropy, meditation, speaking the truth,
> forbearance, forgiveness, and eschewing greed—

these are said to be the eight paths of dharma. (8)

> Of these, the first four pursuits
> may be just to impress the world
> but the last four qualities are to be found
> only in a great soul. (9)

And I have given up greed and covetousness to such an extent that I am willing to donate my own gold bangle to just about anybody. But who cares? It will still be said that tigers only eat men! Because:

> Fixed in their old ways,
> the world will not believe a prostitute
> who may speak about dharma
> but will only believe a Brahmin on the subject
> even if he be a sinner. (10)

Moreover, I have also studied the scriptures on dharma! Hear this:

> Like rain to a desert
> and a meal to one starving
> a gift given to the poor
> is truly effective. (11)

> And just as our life is dear to us
> so too is everyone's life dear to them.
> Hence good people protect the lives of others
> and are kind to them as if to their own selves. (12)

Furthermore:

> In granting a request or withholding one
> in making a donation or not
> in joy and sorrow, in good times and bad,
> a person should think of himself

as if he were in that same position. (13)

And:

> He who regards the wives of others as his own mother
> the wealth of others as akin to a worthless pebble on the road
> and the lives of others just like his own
> he is a true pandit! (14)

And you, oh traveller, are so badly off. That is why I want to give you this gift. For it has been said:

> Serve the needy and not the rich.
> Medicines are of use to those ill
> and not to the healthy! (15)

> Only a gift given wholeheartedly,
> appropriate to the place, time, and worthiness of the recipient
> is a good and auspicious gift. (16)

Therefore, oh traveller, cleanse yourself by bathing in this pond here and then accept this golden bangle from me,' said the tiger. Persuaded thus by the words of the tiger and his own greed, as soon as the traveller entered the pond for a dip, he found himself sinking in the slush and unable to escape. Seeing him stuck, the tiger spoke out: 'Oh dear, you are badly mired in the mud. Let me help you.' Saying so, the tiger advanced slowly on the hapless man and caught hold of him. The poor traveller's last thoughts were:

> 'How does reading the sacred books
> emancipate a villain?
> Nature and temperament are supreme
> in shaping a person.

Just as the nature of cow's milk, which is sweet,
can never be altered. (17)

And:

Those who have no control
over their senses, thoughts, and desires,
their actions yield no fruit
just like an elephant bath
which is followed soon enough by the application of dust anew.
And, in the same way, knowledge without action
is of no use just as ornaments on an ill-tempered woman. (18)

So, I have made a big mistake in trusting a violent-natured beast. It has rightly been said:

Never trust rivers in flow, men with arms,
animals with claws and horns, women,
and relatives of the king! (19)

And further:

Always judge everyone by their temperament
rather than other qualities.
For temperament is paramount! (20)

And:

Even the moon that roams
up above in the sky among the constellations,
emanating a thousand rays of light and chasing away the darkness,
is fated to be eclipsed from time to time.
Who then can erase what is written in one's destiny?' (21)

Even as the traveller mused in this way, he was killed and eaten by the tiger. 'Which is why I, Chitragriva, the king of pigeons, say that it is greed that killed the traveller and it may kill us too. Therefore, one must never act without thinking things through. Because:

> Well-thought words and well-considered actions
> like well-digested food, a well-educated child,
> a well-taught wife, and a well-served king,
> never give bad results.' (22)

Hearing Chitragriva speak thus, a haughty pigeon challenged him with the words: 'What on earth are you saying?

> We should listen to the advice of elders like you
> only in the event of a crisis.
> If we defer to them all the time,
> we will scarcely be able to feed ourselves! (23)

Because:

> There can be doubts
> about everything edible or drinkable on this planet.
> How does one decide what to want and what to give up then?
> Indeed, how does one keep alive then? (24)

> Six types of persons are always unhappy:
> the envious, the resentful, the discontented,
> the wrathful, the dependent,
> and the perpetually suspicious!' (25)

Listening to the words of the haughty pigeon, all the other pigeons descended on the grains of rice as well as the trap laid thereupon. Because:

> Even the learned and those who dispel doubts
> come to grief
> driven by greed and lust. (26)

> Greed gives rise to anger,
> desire, attachment, and ultimately destruction.
> It is thus the cause of sin. (27)

> Despite knowing that a deer made of gold is impossible,
> Lord Rama chased after it.
> When adversity strikes, even the minds of great men
> are compromised. (28)

In this way, all the pigeons were ensnared in the net, and began to condemn the haughty pigeon whose advice they had followed. Thus, it is said:

> Never lead a group into anything.
> If the enterprise succeeds,
> its fruits will be shared by all.
> But if it fails,
> the leader must pay the price! (29)

Hearing their hate-filled words for the haughty pigeon, Chitragriva, the king of the pigeons, said: 'Hey, this is not his fault. Because:

> Even beneficial things
> can occasion setbacks.
> Just as the mother cow's leg itself
> becomes the post to which the calf is shackled. (30)

Besides:

> A friend is one who rescues
> people fallen into trouble.

> One who insults sad people
> instead of finding solutions to their problems
> is no friend at all. (31)

Panic in the event of a crisis is the sign of cowardice. Let us persevere and think of a countermove to the trap.
Because:

> Great people by nature
> exhibit fortitude in times of crisis,
> forgiveness in times of prosperity,
> prowess in battle,
> eloquence in an assembly,
> interest in a good reputation,
> and an unswerving attachment to the scriptures. (32)

> One who does not exult in victory
> nor sorrow in defeat,
> and stands unshakeable in the battlefield,
> such a person is a rare tribute to the three worlds,
> and the mother who gave birth to him is even rarer. (33)

> Indeed, one who wishes to advance in this world
> must give up six weaknesses:
> excess sleep, languor, sloth,
> fear, anger, and verbosity! (34)

Let us do the same now! United, let us lift the net and fly off together. Because:

> When tiny beings come together,
> they can pull off great things!
> Just as a rope made from blades of grass
> can tie down a wild elephant. (35)

> Members of a family sticking together is always beneficial
> even if their numbers are small.
> Since a grain of rice separated from its covering
> stops growing.' (36)

Determining thus, all the birds flew off together with the net! Seeing his net in the sky, the hunter ran after them, thinking to himself:

> 'These birds have flown off with my net.
> But once they descend to the ground,
> I'll have them in my clutches again.' (37)

But once the birds went out of his line of vision, the hunter stopped and returned. Seeing that greedy man going away, the pigeons said: 'What do we do now?'

Chitragriva replied:

> 'Parents and friends are by definition
> our well-wishers.
> Others need some reason or inducement
> to help. (38)

So, I have a friend named Hiranyaka, the king of mice, who lives in the Chitra Forest on the banks of the Gandaki River. He will gladly bite through our net.' Thinking thus, all the birds approached Hiranyaka's burrow. Canny Hiranyaka had put a hundred gates in his burrow to keep out any lurking predators. Hearing the whooshing sound of the birds all descending together, Hiranyaka was frightened and sat quietly inside. So Chitragriva called out: 'Oh friend Hiranyaka! Why won't you speak to us?' Hiranyaka recognized his voice and slowly emerged from the ground and said: 'Oh, I am blessed! It is my dear friend Chitragriva!

> Those who are in regular touch with their friends,
> share confidences with them,
> and hang out with them often,
> they are the luckiest people in the world!' (39)

Then, seeing them trapped in the snare, he was quiet a moment, and then asked: 'Goodness, buddy, what is this?'

Chitragriva replied: 'Oh friend, this is the fruit of our bad karma in a previous birth.

> Whatever we do, whenever and wherever we do it,
> and in whatever way we do it,
> in precisely the same way, the same thing, and for the same duration,
> we bear the results of our actions. (40)

> Disease, grief, regret,
> detention and calamities—
> these are all the fruits
> borne by the tree of our crimes.' (41)

Hearing him speak thus, Hiranyaka rushed to cut Chitragriva's shackles. Chitragriva cried out: 'No, no! Please don't. First cut the snare around the feet of the other pigeons, who are my responsibility. Later you can cut mine.' But Hiranyaka said to him: 'Buddy, my teeth are too delicate to cut through so much net. Let me cut through your snare till my teeth last. Then, if I still can, I will do the others too.' Chitragriva spoke: 'Hmm, okay, I understand. But even so, please cut their snare first as best as you can.' Hiranyaka replied: 'Sacrificing yourself to protect your dependents defies the logic of prudent conduct. Because:

> One should save money for times of need.
> With it one should save one's wife.

And with both money and wife,
one should save oneself at all times! (42)

Further:

Staying alive is necessary
to pursue piety, power, pleasure, and salvation.
If you give up your life, you give up all these.
And if you protect your life,
you protect the world and beyond.' (43)

Then Chitragriva spoke: 'Friend, you are right, prudent conduct does so dictate. But I am personally incapable of seeing my dependents in distress. This is why I made that request. Since:

The wise should sacrifice their wealth
and even their lives
for the good of others.
Death is inevitable,
so why not die for the sake of good people? (44)

And, I have another reason too:
These pigeons and I bear the same qualities,
whether it is species, possessions, or strength.
What then will set me apart from them as their king?
When else will I have the opportunity
to prove my leadership
if not now? (45)

Moreover:

Their loyalty to me
is not from any selfish motives.
So, please do save their lives
even at the cost of mine! (46)

My body is an impermanent mass of flesh and bones,
faeces, and urine.
Shed your attachment to it
and further my glory instead, my friend! (47)

Indeed, if from this destructible and filth-laden body,
I can obtain pure and ever-lasting glory,
what more can I ask for? (48)

Because:

The body is perishable
while good qualities
last till the end of time!' (49)

Hearing these words, Hiranyaka was elated. He said: 'Wonderful, oh friend, wonderful! By your love for your dependents, you have shown that you are deserving of the kingship of all three worlds.' And then he proceeded to quickly cut away the shackles of all the birds. Then, after greeting them, he spoke again: 'Friend Chitragriva, do not blame yourself for what happened with the net and the trap. Because:

While birds can spy a tiny morsel of food
from miles away,
they cannot spot the gross knots of a snare
when bad luck approaches. (50)

If you think about how the sun and the moon
are eclipsed by the planets,
or a mighty elephant and a dangerous snake
come to be captured and caged,
or an intelligent person suffers poverty and destitution,
the only explanation seems to be
that fate is supreme. (51)

Which is why:

> Even birds flying up above in the sky
> or fish swimming deep within the sea
> still get caught and die.
> Which place then is free from danger,
> and what does good or bad conduct amount to?
> Death sits in wait and can grab
> who it wants even on the off-chance.' (52)

Consoling his guests in this fashion, Hiranyaka extended hospitality to them and then saw them off. Chitragriva and his family returned to their land, and Hiranyaka too re-entered his burrow.

> Thus, we must make lots of friends,
> no matter what kind.
> See how through the friendship of the mouse,
> the pigeons were freed from their shackles! (53)

Now, Laghupatnaka, the crow, who had witnessed the entire episode, spoke with amazement: 'Oh Hiranyaka! You are worthy of praise. Now I too want to befriend you, so kindly accept my offer of friendship.' Hearing this, Hiranyaka replied from within his burrow: 'But who are you?' The crow said: 'I am Laghupatnaka, the crow.'

Hiranyaka laughed out loud and said: 'There can be no friendship with you! Because:

> The wise only match things
> that are equal and deserving of each other.
> But you, a crow, are the predator and I, a mouse, the prey.
> How can there ever be love between us? (54)

In fact, the friendship of the prey and predator
can only prove disastrous.
That's how the deer was trapped by the jackal,
and had to be rescued by the crow.' (55)

Laghupatnaka asked: 'How did that happen?' So, Hiranyaka started to narrate.

THE THIRD STORY

In the land of Magadha there is a great forest called Champakavati. There lived two old and dear friends, a crow and a deer. Once a jackal caught sight of the deer who was stout with good health and roamed here and there at will. And he thought to himself: 'Now, how should I get a taste of this delicious meal? Ah, let me first win his trust.' Accordingly he went up to the deer and said: 'Hi. How are you?' The deer asked: 'Who are you?'

He replied: 'I am a jackal named Kshudrabuddhi (Lowly Mind). Without any friends, I live a hellish life in this forest. Now that I have found you, I am no longer friendless and so happy am I that I will remain your devoted servant till the end of my days.' The deer agreed, and as the sun set, the two returned to the deer's home, where his close friend, the crow named Subuddhi (Good Sense), was perched atop a champa tree branch.

Seeing the two of them, the crow asked: 'Hey, who is this other person?' The deer replied: 'He is a jackal and wants to be friends with us.' The crow said: 'Buddy! You should not make friends with someone who has suddenly shown up. For it has been said:

Never allow in your home a stranger
whose background or nature you know nothing of.

That's exactly how the old vulture died
at the hands of the cat.' (56)

In response, both the deer and the jackal exclaimed: 'How so?' Then the crow began to narrate.

THE FOURTH STORY

On the banks of the Bhagirathi River, atop the Gridhrakuta Mountain, there is a giant fig tree. In the hollow of the tree there lived an old and blind vulture by the name of Jaradgava (Old One) whose nails had dissolved with age. He subsisted on the leavings the other avian residents of the tree fed him out of compassion. One day, a cat named Dirghakarna (Long Ear) arrived with a view to eat the birds' young ones. Seeing him, the babies began to loudly chirp with fear. Hearing them, Jaradgava boldly asked: 'Who is it?' When Dirghakarna noticed the vulture, he panicked. Because:

'Fear is possible
only till the danger is afar.
Once it is right in front of you,
you should do exactly what is needed. (57)

I can't run away from him now. So, whatever happens, let it happen. And let me first try to win his trust.'

With that thought the cat went up to the vulture and said: 'Salutations to you, oh noble one!' The vulture asked: 'Who are you?' He replied: I am a cat.' The vulture shot back: 'Get away from here! Or I will kill you.' The cat, however, calmly replied: 'First just listen to me. And then if I still deserve to be killed, kill me.

Because:

> Is a person worthy of being killed or revered
> merely because of his background?
> First evaluate his conduct
> and then let him be killed or worshipped.' (58)

The vulture then said: 'Go on, say why you have come here.' Dirghakarna replied: 'I come here regularly to bathe on the holy banks of the Ganga. I am a student of the scriptures and do not eat meat. I am practising the Chandrayan fast these days. All birds always praise me as one who is pious, learned, and worthy of their trust. You are senior to me not only in age but also in knowledge, so I have come here to learn from you, oh blessed one. You are keen to kill your guest. But it is becoming of a householder to:

> Honour even an enemy
> if he comes as a guest to your house.
> Just as a tree does not withhold its shade
> even from the woodcutter. (59)

If you lack resources to take care of him, at least shower him with sweet words of hospitality. Because:

> A comfortable seat, a glass of water,
> and sweet and true words
> are never lacking
> in the homes of good people. (60)

> They are kind even to people
> who lack good qualities.
> Just as moonlight shines
> even on the homes of sinners. (61)

Further:

> Should a guest be turned away,
> disappointed, he leaves behind his sins
> and takes away the merits
> of the host. (62)
>
> If a person of a low caste arrives
> at the house of someone from a high caste,
> he must still be taken good care of
> because every guest is akin to God.' (63)

The vulture then spoke: 'A cat is always fond of meat. And here live the little ones of many a bird. That's the only reason I threatened you.'

Hearing this, the cat reverentially touched the ground and then his ears, and said: 'I am in the middle of practising the rigorous Chandrayan ritual which is prescribed by the holy scriptures. And the scriptures, despite other debates therein, all maintain that non-violence is the greatest virtue. Because:

> Those who forsake violence of every kind,
> endure all difficulties,
> and protect everyone else—
> they attain heaven. (64)
>
> Virtue alone accompanies one
> on the journey after death.
> Every other possession is left behind
> with the mortal body. (65)
>
> See how unequal are
> the one who eats the flesh of another
> and that poor creature who is eaten:
> while for one it is a moment of pleasure,

for the other, it is the end of the world. (66)

Nobody else can understand
and describe the anguish of
one who knows
he is about to die! (67)

So, listen! When one can readily survive on vegetables,
why incur the tremendous sin
of taking another's life?' (68)

Thus dispelling suspicions and winning trust, the cat began to live in the hollow of the tree. And before long, he began to steal the little bird babies and eat them quietly inside his hollow. The bird parents who lost their young in this way started to weep and desperately search for the missing children. At this, the cat left his burrow and ran away.

Soon after, the parents discovered inside the burrow the bones of the babies that had been eaten alive. They instantly blamed the vulture and screamed: 'This Jaradgava has eaten our children!' Convinced of the truth of this, all the other birds got together and killed the old vulture.

'And this is why I say,' said the wise crow to his friend, the deer, 'do not befriend one you know nothing about.'

Annoyed at this, the jackal shot back: 'The day you met this deer, your nature and background too were unknown. How come the two of you became friends then?

Indeed, in the absence of learned people
even the semi-literate gain a reputation!
Just as in arid lands where no trees grow,
even the castor oil palm is considered a tree! (69)

In any case, this is mine and that belongs to another

only the small-minded think in this way.
For the magnanimous,
the whole world is one family. (70)

So, just like I consider this deer my friend, I consider you too.'

The deer now said: 'What is to be gained from this argument? Let us all live together in peace and mutual trust. Because:

Nobody is a friend or an enemy per se.
It is one's behaviour that produces
friends or enemies.' (71)

'Very well,' said the crow.

Then one day, the jackal spoke to the deer in private: 'Buddy, come, let me show you this lush field full of grain elsewhere in this forest.' The deer followed him that day and then went grazing in that field every day.

Soon enough, the owner of the field laid a trap and the next time the poor deer went there, he was caught. He then fervently thought: 'Who but a friend can save me from this deathlike noose?' Just then the jackal came that way and gleefully observed below his breath: 'My plan worked! Now I can eat his flesh, drink his blood, and gnaw at his bones to my heart's desire'. The poor deer's spirits, on the other hand, rose when he saw the jackal, and he said: 'Hey, buddy, cut my noose and set me free quick! Because:

The real test of a friend
is in times of crisis,
like the test of a warrior is in battle,
of honesty in debt, of a woman in poverty,
and of relatives in grief. (72)

Moreover:

They who stick by your side
in celebration and mourning alike,
whether in famine or prosperity,
in the cemetery or the king's palace—
they alone are friends.' (73)

The jackal meanwhile was staring at the noose knot. 'It's tied rather tightly,' he thought. Then he spoke aloud: 'Listen, pal, your noose is made out of sinews. I can't possibly put my mouth to it on a holy Sunday, can I? If you don't mind, let me return tomorrow morning and do your bidding.' The jackal then went and hid himself not far away.

In the meanwhile, not finding the deer back home even after dusk, the crow set out to search for him, and soon chanced upon the trapped one. He exclaimed: 'Oh no, what the hell is this, my friend?!' The deer sadly replied: 'The result of not listening to one's friend. Thus it is said:

He who doesn't listen to the advice
of a well-meaning friend
invites calamities on himself
and much gratification for his enemies.' (74).

The crow exclaimed: 'Where is that fraud jackal?' The deer replied: 'Desirous of my flesh, he must be around here somewhere.' The crow burst out: 'I told you so!

Just because you have done someone no harm
is no reason to trust they will not harm you either.
Good people always have reason to fear the bad
who do not care for virtue and vice. (75)

Friends who speak sweetly to your face
but sabotage you behind your back,

much like a bowl of milk laced with poison,
should be abandoned forthwith.' (76)

The crow then sighed deeply and spoke: 'Oh, you fraud! What do you think you have achieved?

> Do you think it is a big deal
> to trick the decent, the trapped, the hopeful,
> the trusting, and the needy? (77)

> Oh Mother Earth, how do you bear such villains
> who deceive the honest,
> the generous, and the innocent? (78)

> Never ever befriend a crook!
> For when hot, an ember will burn your hand,
> and even after cooling down,
> it will still blacken it. (79)

> Villains behave like mosquitoes!
> They first fall at the feet and attempt to please.
> Then they back-bite!
> They hum all things strange and wonderful in your ears,
> and then, when they are well positioned,
> they sting! (80)

> A crook speaking sweetly is no reason to trust him.
> He will have honey on his lips
> but deadly poison fills his heart.' (81)

The next morning the crow saw the owner of the field approach, stick in hand. He turned to the deer: 'Friend, listen, play dead! Lie still and bloat your stomach and pull in your legs. Then, when I give the sign, get up and run!'

The deer obeyed and pretended to be dead. The owner

was pleased that the deed was already done. He loosened and removed the noose and began to wrap up the net. This was the moment the crow was waiting for: he gave the signal and the deer shot up and ran for his life!
Astonished and frustrated, the owner threw his stick with all his might, which went and struck the jackal in hiding, and he died.

Thus, it is said:

> You are served just desserts
> for good deeds and bad
> whenever they get too much,
> whether it is in three years, three months,
> three fortnights, or three days. (82)

Anyway, this is why I say friendship between prey and predator is never a good idea. Again the crow said:

> If I eat you, it will hardly satiate my hunger.
> But if I let you live, my fame and I will live through you,
> just as the virtuous Chitragriva said. (83)

And:

> Even birds and animals trust a man of virtue.
> Because such a man
> never changes his disposition. (84)

> Even if he is angry,
> the goodness of his nature will never change.
> Just like the ocean's temperature
> does not rise
> from burning matchsticks. (85)

Hiranyaka, the king of mice, then said to Laghupatnaka: 'You, oh crow, are flighty. And one should never love a flighty person.

For it has been said:

> A cat, a buffalo, a sheep, a crow,
> and a mean-minded person
> bully and dominate once you show them affection.
> Never trust any of these, therefore. (86)

Also, you are a natural enemy of mine. And it is said that:

> Never make friends or sign a treaty
> with an enemy, no matter how sweetly they behave.
> For no matter how hot the water is
> it will always put out fire. (87)

> Even if a crook be learned,
> he should be forsaken.
> For a jewel-bearing serpent
> is still a terrifying thing! (88)

> An impossibility can never come to pass,
> only the possible can still happen.
> Thus, a cart cannot move on water
> and a boat cannot sail on land. (89)

> And he who goes out of his way to trust
> enemies and disenchanted wives
> approaches his end!' (90)

Laghupatnaka then said: 'All right, I heard everything you said. I have nonetheless decided I want to be friends with you. Otherwise, I will starve myself to death.

> See, friendship with wicked people
> is like an earthen pot,
> easy to break and difficult to repair.
> But with a good person,

> it is like a golden pot,
> hard to break and if broken,
> easy to meld back in shape. (91)
>
> And while metals come together from melting,
> birds and animals for some purpose (like hunting or having children),
> and fools out of fear and greed,
> good people can recognize each other and unite
> just on sight. (92)

Further:

> Friends are like coconuts,
> hard on the outside and soft and sweet on the inside.
> Others are like jujubes,
> attractive only on the outside. (93)
>
> Even after a break-up,
> good people do not change their kind ways.
> Just as the fibres of a lotus stalk broken in two
> still cling on. (94)
>
> Other qualities of a friend include
> straightforwardness, generosity,
> bravery, equanimity,
> attachment, and honesty. (95)

Now, if not you, where else will I find a friend like this?'

Pleased at his sweet words, Hiranyaka came out of his burrow and said: 'I feel great hearing you. For it has been said:

> Nothing pleases the heart more
> than the affectionate and attractive words
> spoken by a good person.

> Not even a bath in cold water,
> a salve of sandalwood paste
> or a necklace of pearls
> feels as good to one sunburnt. (96)

Further:

> Things that spoil a friendship include
> divulging secrets, borrowing money,
> harshness, skittishness,
> anger, lies, and gambling. (97)

But from your words you don't seem to have any of these tendencies.
   And:

> Eloquence and truthfulness
> become apparent from speech.
> While humility and pacifism
> can be known only through actions. (98)

Further:

> Friendship with a sincere person
> just feels special
> whereas the speech of one whose intentions are corrupt
> sounds very different. (99)

> The thoughts, the words, and the actions of a good person
> are all the same and in sync.
> Whereas a wicked man thinks one thing,
> says out loud another, and goes and actually does
> something altogether different. (100)

So okay, sure, let your wish prevail.'
   Speaking thus, Hiranyaka agreed to be friends with

Laghupatnaka, fed him an assortment of fine dishes, and then re-entered his burrow. The crow too went home. Ever after this these two would check on each other's well-being from time to time, exchange good food, and make sound conversation.

Once Laghupatnaka said: 'It's hard to get food here, really. I want to move.' Hiranyaka asked him where he wanted to go. For it has been said:

> The wise move forward but hesitantly.
> For without ascertaining your destination,
> it is best not to leave home. (101)

The crow replied: 'Oh I have checked out this place.'

'Where is it?' asked Hiranyaka.

'There is a lake called Karpurgaur in the Dandak, or the southern forest. A very decent tortoise called Manthara, who lives in that lake, is a long-time friend of mine. Because:

> Rare are the people [like him]
> who actually perform their duties.
> Most will just advise others to do so,
> which is always easy. (102)

Rest assured, Manthara will ply me with different delicacies and take good care of me.'

> Hiranyaka then spoke: 'What will I do here alone then?
> Where you have no respect, no livelihood, no friend,
> and do not grow in wisdom and learning,
> such a place is best given up. (103)

What's more:

> One should not stay at a place
> where you can't earn a living

or where freedom from fear is not to be found,
nor modesty, goodness, and liberality. (104)

And, further, friend, one should not stay
where there is no moneylender, doctor,
teacher of the Veda,
or a river with clean water. (105)

So, please take me along too.'

The two friends then chatted their way to the Karpurgaur Lake. Manthara spotted his friend from afar and showed great hospitality to him and the mouse. Because

Whoever comes home must be served well,
be it a child, a young man, or an elder.
For all guests are venerable. (106)

The sacrificial fire is venerable for the Brahmin,
the Brahmin is venerable for all four castes,
a husband is venerable for his wife,
and a guest is venerable for all. (107)

The crow addressed his friend: 'Dear Manthara, please take extra care of Hiranyaka, he is the king of mice and a very kind and noble soul. Even the two thousand tongues of Shesha, the divine serpent, cannot do justice to praising his qualities.' Saying so, he narrated the entire episode with Chitragriva. Manthara deferred greatly to Hiranyaka and then asked: 'But, pray, what is the reason for your visit to this distant forest?' Hiranyaka proceeded to narrate.

THE FIFTH STORY

In a city called Champak, there once was a settlement of ascetics. There lived Chudakarna (Moon-ear), a mendicant. At the end of the day, he would hang up on a nail his begging bowl together with the leftovers of alms he had received. I used to jump up onto the bowl and eat those leavings.

Then one day his friend Vinakarna (Lute-ear) arrived. While Vinakarna was chatting with him, telling many wondrous tales, Chudakarna was busy trying to chase me away from his alms bowl by repeatedly striking the floor with a long bamboo pole. Vinakarna then asked: 'Whatever is the matter, friend? You seem least interested in my stories and much more so in something else.'

Chudakarna replied: 'No, I am not uninterested. It's just that there is this mouse who troubles me by leaping into the bowl and eating all the grain therein.' Vinakarna was amazed. He said: 'How can such a tiny mouse leap so high? There is more than meets the eye here. Just like when:

> The young woman all of a sudden held tight
> and passionately kissed
> her aging husband.
> There had to be some explanation!' (108)

Chudakarna went: 'What was that now?' So, Vinakarna began to narrate.

THE SIXTH STORY

Kaushambi is a city in the province of Gaud, or Bengal. There lived a rich merchant called Chandandasa. Driven by lust in his old age and the power of his wealth, he married the young daughter of another merchant, by the name of Lilavati. She was a deeply sensuous woman but the old man could hardly satiate her. Because:

> Women have no interest in husbands
> with old and weathered organs.
> Just like those with frostbite
> don't care for the moon
> and those with sunburn
> look away from the sun. (109)

> Aged men are hardly virile.
> Their wives are taken with other men
> and regard the husband
> as a necessary evil, just like medicine. (110)

But that old man was besotted with her. Because:

> While living beings lust for life and wealth,
> the aged desire a young wife
> more than life itself! (111)

> An old man can neither enjoy sense-pleasures
> nor renounce them!
> Like an old, toothless dog who cannot chew the bone,
> but helplessly licks at it. (112)

Soon passion drove Lilavati to forsake her family's reputation and enter into a relationship with another merchant's son. Because:

> Women are driven to ruin in this way
> because of any of the following reasons:
> excessive liberty, indiscipline, late marriage,
> meeting someone at a festival
> or on a trip, chatting intimately with a man,
> living abroad, the company of immoral women,
> repeated transgressions, an aging husband, an envious one,
> or one who has gone away on work to distant lands. (113)

The following habits also spoil women:
drinking liquor, company of bad characters,
separation from the husband, vagrant wanderings,
and staying the night at the place of another. (114)

In fact, it is only in the absence
of an opportune place, time, and person to seduce them
that feminine chastity is preserved! (115)

Women do not love or hate anyone.
They just look for new men
as cows in the pasture
look for new grass! (116)

Women are like a pot of clarified butter
and men are like a burning ember.
Use your brains!
Don't keep butter and fire close together. (117)

In fact, men must not stay alone
with their own mother, sister, or daughter,
for sense-pleasures are very powerful
and can snare even the wise. (118)

Neither modesty nor decorum,
good sense nor fear
keeps women chaste.
It is only the absence of a suitor that does. (119)

A woman never attains freedom.
Her father protects her in childhood,
husband in her youth,
and son in her old age. (120)

Once Lilavati was sitting happily, chatting away with her lover on her beautiful bed. Suddenly her husband came home! She got up in a trice, grabbed him passionately, and started kissing him furiously. Thus, her lover was able to escape unnoticed. And so, it is said:

> All the learning of the great teachers
> Shukra and Brihaspati
> is already spontaneously known
> to a woman! (121)

A bawd nearby who saw this scene wondered how a young woman could behave so amorously with an old man. When she got to know the truth, she scolded her in private. Hence, I gave the example of Lilavati and the old man. In the same way, there must be an explanation for this mouse's feat.

Vinakarna thought for a minute and then said: 'The reason must be an excess of wealth. Because:

> Wealth alone is the source of all power
> everywhere and every time.
> The king's sovereignty too
> rests on wealth. (122)

So then he took a spade and dug up my burrow and confiscated all my stored wealth. Later Chudakarna saw me weak and fearful, moving about slowly, unable to feed myself. So, he said:

> 'Wealth alone is the source of all strength
> and even wisdom in this world.
> Look at this wretched mouse,
> reduced to a shadow of himself now! (123)

> Without wealth, all deeds of a man of low intellect
> come to nought.

Just like streams and rivulets dry up
in the heat of summer. (124)

The wealthy alone are feted and celebrated
in this world.
They alone have all the friends and relatives
and are declared great pandits. (125)

A house without a child is lonesome.
A person without a friend is too.
The directions a fool may head in are pointless.
And everything is pointless for the poor. (126)

Indeed, between poverty and death,
death is better.
You suffer but once when you die.
In poverty there is no end to the suffering. (127)

The same person, with the same name,
brains, and eloquence,
is suddenly transformed completely
without the power of wealth behind him.' (128)

Hiranyaka said: 'Hearing all this I decided it is not right for me to stay here any longer. It wasn't possible to share my plight with anyone either, since:

An intelligent person
should never disclose to another
the loss of his wealth, the grief in his heart,
insults, misdemeanours by his family, or being cheated. (129)

Indeed, one's age, assets, and family secrets,
sexual activities, medication, penance and donations,
and insults received
should be carefully guarded from the public eye. (130)

> In any case, when we fail in endeavours to sustain ourselves
> and luck is turned against us,
> it is best that a poor, forbearing person
> go away somewhere to a forest. (131)
>
> A person of character would rather die
> than crib and complain about his plight
> for even after a fire dies out,
> it does not lose its heat. (132)
>
> And like a bunch of flowers,
> a good man has only two options:
> to adorn someone's head and prosper
> or wilt away in some grove. (133)

And a life of begging is no option at all for him. Because:

> It is better to jump into a fire and die
> than to give up self-respect
> and ask for alms
> from mean people. (134)
>
> Poverty gives rise to shame, shame puts an end to talent,
> absence of talent brings on humiliation,
> humiliation sorrows the heart,
> sorrow renders one unable to use one's mind,
> and loss of the mind destroys a person eventually.
> Alas! Poverty is the root of all calamities! (135)

Further:

> It is better to keep quiet than to lie.
> Better to be a eunuch than to elope with the wife of another.

Better dead than involved with a villain.
And better to eat alms than to feast on stolen wealth.
(136)

Better to have an empty cowshed than to keep a violent bull.
Better a prostitute than a family woman gone astray.
Better to live in a jungle than in the city of a mindless king.
And better dead than in the company of the wicked. (137)

What's more:

Just as servitude robs you of respect
and moonlight robs the night of darkness
and age robs you of looks
and listening to the stories of the gods Vishnu and Shiva robs you of your sins,
so too does begging for help rob you of a hundred innate strengths.' (138)

Hiranyaka continued: 'And how can I live off the food of others? This thought tormented me. Because:

Superficial learning, paid sex, and borrowed food,
these three activities
are ironic and pointless. (139)

And, an ailing person, a person who is away from home for ages,
one who sponges off others for food, and piles on at another's place of stay,
life is akin to death for such people,
and death is release.' (140)

Then Hiranyaka said: 'Although I knew all this, greed led me to try to hoard his wealth yet again. It is said:

> Greed sets one's brains whirring.
> Greed alone fuels want and desire.
> Desire brings disappointment
> and such aggrieved people
> pay a price in this world and the next. (141)

But once Vinakarna spotted me approach slowly and threw a dead bamboo log at me. Then I realized:

> One who knows no contentment
> lands up in all kinds of trouble.
> Lusting after wealth, he sulks all the time
> and loses all sense of balance. (142)

> While one who is content at heart
> wins all the riches of the world.
> Like one wearing leather shoes
> feels all roads are lined with leather! (143)

> Indeed! One quenched with the elixir of contentment
> knows a joy
> that none who runs after wealth
> can ever obtain. (144)

> And he who renounces all desires
> and finds contentment,
> he is the true master
> and he the true practitioner! (145)

> Blessed is he who
> has never had to beg the rich for help,
> or know the pain of separation in love,
> or speak piteous words of desperation. (146)

> One who lusts will go to any lengths and troubles
> for fulfilment.
> But one who is content will hardly celebrate
> even if riches drop in his lap. (147)

Therefore, one must act according to the circumstances.

> In this world, what is dharma? It is compassion.
> What is happiness? It is freedom from disease.
> What is affection? It is goodwill.
> And what is wisdom? It is discerning action. (148)

> Discerning action alone is wisdom
> in times of adversity.
> Those who don't think and act
> face challenges at every step. (149)

Further:

> If needed, abandon one person for the sake of the family,
> abandon the family for the sake of the village,
> and abandon the village for the sake of the country.
> But for the sake of yourself, renounce the world itself! (150)

> And, if one has to choose between water
> that is freely available
> and food that is served as a favour,
> it is better to opt for that which
> brings peace of mind. (151)

Having thought about all this, I have come to this desolate forest,' said Hiranyaka. 'Because:

> It is better to sleep under a tree
> on the grass in this forest teeming with wild animals
> and eat roots and fruits and wear clothes made of bark

than to live in poverty amidst your kin. (152)

Then by sheer good luck, my friend Laghupatnaka showered me with affection and now you, Manthara, have taken me in with such respect. It feels like heaven! Because:

> There are only two kinds of pleasures
> worth experiencing in this world.
> The sweetness of poetry
> and the company of good people.' (153)

Now Manthara the tortoise spoke:

> 'Money is like the dust that gathers on our feet.
> Youth is like a stream gushing in the mountains.
> Age is fickle like a bubble on water
> And life itself is ephemeral like foam.
> So, the fool who does not perform his righteous duties,
> which open the gates to heaven,
> lives to repent and grieve in his old age. (154)

You, Hiranyaka, hoarded a lot. This is the result of that. For, listen:

> To donate your earnings from time to time is sensible.
> Just as draining an overflowing tank every now and then
> makes for safety. (155)

> And if you bury hoarded wealth too deep under the earth
> it finds its way into the netherworld! (156)

> And he who does not enjoy his wealth
> but labours just to pile it up,
> he is no better off than a slave
> and suffers like one. (157)

> If a rich man doesn't enjoy or donate his wealth
> how is he better off than us?
> We are just as rich! (158)
>
> A miser who does not give his wealth
> to the gods, Brahmins, and to his friends and family in need
> his wealth is either stolen or confiscated by the king
> or lost in a fire someday. (159)
>
> Money can only be enjoyed,
> given in charity, or lost.
> He who does not give or spend
> must see his wealth destroyed. (160)
>
> A miser's unspent wealth
> is as good as belonging to another,
> for it brings him no joy.
> But if his riches are lost,
> it is he alone who grieves and suffers. (161)
>
> Rare in this world are these four:
> donation with a smile,
> knowledge without conceit,
> valour accompanied by mercy,
> and money assigned for charity. (162)

Thus, it is said:

> Certainly save money but do not hoard it.
> Look what happened to the jackal who hoarded wealth:
> he was shot dead.' (163)

'What happened?!' asked the crow and the mouse. Manthara then began to narrate.

THE SEVENTH STORY

In a village called Kalyana, there lived a hunter by the name of Bhairava. One day, in search of deer, he went towards the Vindhya Forest. Having successfully felled a deer, Bhairava was dragging off the carcass when he suddenly saw a terrifying boar. Putting the carcass down, Bhairava shot the boar too. The boar roared and charged at Bhairava, striking him in his groin. Bhairava fell dead.

> Indeed, water, fire, poison, arms,
> hunger, disease, and a fall from a mountain—
> a person may die of any of these causes. (164)

As a result of their scuffle, a serpent on the ground was also killed. Soon a jackal named Dirgharava, who was scouting for food, passed by, and seeing the dead deer, hunter, boar, and snake, thought to himself: 'Oh wow, what a spread ready for me!

> Just as unforeseen sorrows befall people,
> so do great joys.
> I do believe fate is supreme in these matters. (165)

Anyway, the flesh of these four will last me a good three months!

> The man will sustain me for a month, the deer and the
> boar for another month each, and the serpent for a day.
> Today, however, let me start with chewing on the hunter's
> bowstring made of sinew!' (166)

As he began to chew on the string, however, the bow snapped suddenly and struck him hard on the chest, piercing it. Dirgharava died on the spot.

'This is why I say save wealth but do not hoard,' said

Manthara. 'It has been said, after all:

> Wealth used for charity or for one's own enjoyment,
> that alone is wealth.
> Otherwise, after death, others will toy with our assets
> as they will with our wife. (167)

> So, I believe that whatever you use or give
> to worthy recipients, that alone is your wealth.
> The rest actually belongs to others
> and you are only safeguarding it for them! (168)

Anyway, let bygones be bygones. Because:

> The wise do not lust for the unattainable.
> They do not grieve for what is destroyed.
> And they do not form attachments in times of adversity.
> (169)

So, dear friend, may you now live happily forever. Because:

> You can read all the scriptures but remain a fool.
> The one who acts on his learning is the true scholar.
> Just like good medicine does not work
> by taking its name alone
> it must act to cure the sick. (170)

Further:

> Learning does not help one
> who is afraid to act.
> Just as a lamp held by a blind man
> cannot show him the way. (171)

So, friend, make your peace with your new circumstances. It should not be difficult either, because:

Only cowards say never leave your place
or that a king, a bride, a Brahmin, and a minister,
the breasts, the teeth, the hair, and the nails
and humans in general
don't look good out of place! (172)

In fact, lions, elephants, and great persons
all leave their places and roam.
Only crows, deer, and cowards
die where they were born! (173)

For the brave and the capable,
what is the difference between home and abroad?
They triumph and flourish wherever they go!
Just as a lion kills and hunts
in every new forest he goes. (174)

And just like frogs and birds
are inexorably drawn to lakes and pools
so too do all good things
come to industrious people. (175)

In any case, one must put up with joy and sorrow
for only when one goes will the other come. (176)

And one who is enthusiastic, hard-working, well-trained,
brave, grateful, and without vices but with friends—
Lakshmi, the goddess of fortune, blesses him
automatically. (177)

The best thing is that a brave man, even if without wealth,
can attain positions of high stature.
But a coward, even if wealthy, can never win respect.
Just as a dog may wear a golden necklace
but cannot acquire the lustre of a grand lion. (178)

Why do people pride themselves on wealth anyway?
Or feel ashamed of their poverty?
These states of human existence go up and down
just like a juggling ball. (179)

Moreover:

> Wealth, just like the shade of a cloud,
> or the love of a villain, new grain, women, and youth,
> is meant to be enjoyed but fleetingly. (180)

> So, one shouldn't stress too much over one's livelihood.
> It's already taken care of by God.
> Just like the mother's milk begins to flow
> as soon as the baby is born. (181)

> So, friend, He who made the parrot green, the swan white
> and the peacock multicoloured,
> He will assure your livelihood too. (182)

And listen to this secret:

> The wealth you have to slave to earn,
> and grieve for, when lost,
> and lose your sense of balance when obtained—
> how can such wealth bring happiness? (183)

What's more:

> Those who want wealth for righteous purposes
> would do well not to lust for it at all.
> Because it is better to not wade into slush
> than to have to wash it off later! (184)

Because:

> Just as predators abound

on the earth, in the sea, and the skies,
so too do dangers abound
for the wealthy. (185)

The king, water, fire,
thieves, and relatives alike—
the wealthy live in constant fear of these.
Just as living beings fear death. (186)

And:

There are worries enough in this lifetime
than to want to court the sorrow
of not having the possessions you crave.
That craving is without end. (187)

Listen further, brother!

It's hard to earn wealth.
And harder still to protect it, once earned.
And once lost, it feels like death.
So do not fret and chase after wealth! (188)

Once you renounce desire,
the rich and the poor are all the same.
But if you let desires in,
they will enslave you in the blink of an eye. (189)

The more one desires an object,
the more that desire grows.
So only that object can be truly attained
which one no longer desires! (190)

Okay, let's not say any more on this! Please stay here with me and pass your time. Because:

The affection of a great soul lasts a lifetime
while his anger is but momentary
and his favours
are without strings attached!' (191)

Hearing this Laghupatnaka exclaimed: 'Oh Manthara, you are wonderful! No praise is too great for your qualities.

Only the good have the ability to rescue the good.
An elephant mired in a swamp
can only be rescued by other elephants. (192)

They alone are praiseworthy in this world
who do not disappoint those in need.' (193)

Then the crow, the mouse, and the tortoise began to live with abandon, eating what they chose and roaming where they pleased.

One day, a deer named Chitranga arrived, all panicked. Seeing his condition, Manthara feared the worst and leapt into the lake. The mouse too entered his burrow and the crow flew up to a treetop. After a while Laghupatnaka decided that there was no danger. Hearing him call out, the other two also emerged and regrouped there. Manthara then addressed Chitranga: 'Is all well, deer? It's good to see you. Don't hesitate to stay in this forest and eat and drink as you wish.' Chitranga spoke: 'I have fled here out of fear of a hunter and seek refuge and friendship with you.' Hiranyaka said: 'We have already become friends, wouldn't you say? Because:

Friends are of four kinds:
those by birth, namely our parents;
those by marriage, namely relatives;
those by inheritance, namely age-old ties;

and those by rescue, namely those who save us from
calamities. (194)

So please make yourself at home here.' Hearing these words, the deer was reassured. He ate and drank as needed and then flopped down under the shade of a tree on the banks of the lake. Then Manthara spoke: 'Tell us, buddy. Why are you running scared in this desolate forest? Are hunters on the prowl?'

The deer replied: 'There is a king called Rukmangada in the country of Kalinga. Out on an expedition to conquer the four quarters, he and his armed forces have stopped by the river Chandrabhaga. And tomorrow morning he will come here and set up camp on the banks of this Karpura Lake. I overheard the hunters speaking of this. So, to stay on here is also a cause of worry. We need to act fast.' Afraid again, the tortoise said he was moving to another lake. The crow and the deer agreed. Only Hiranyaka laughed and said: 'Once the tortoise reaches the other lake, he will be safe. But how will he stay safe while crawling all the way on land? Because:

> Aquatic animals rely heavily on water,
> as do fort-dwellers on the fort,
> tigers and other animals on the land,
> and the king on his minister. (195)

Oh Laghupatnaka, this advice will create a situation like:

> When the merchant's son
> was saddened on seeing
> his wife's soft breasts
> pressed hard.' (196)

'What?' the other two exclaimed. Hiranyaka began to narrate.

THE EIGHTH STORY

There was in the kingdom of Kanyakubja a king named Virasena. He had set up a prince called Tungbala as his heir apparent in a town called Virpur. Once, that wealthy young man was wandering in the town, when he came upon the young and sensuous bride of a merchant. He returned to his palace all aroused and then sent a female messenger to her. Because:

> Men stay on the straight and narrow path
> controlling their senses
> and behaving with modesty
> only till such time as they are not
> exposed to the deeply distracting attraction
> of a beautiful damsel's glance. (197)

That beauty too was lost in thoughts of him ever since she set eyes on the prince. As it has been said:

> Lies, lust, boldness, deception,
> a lack of qualities and of purity
> come naturally to women! (198)

Hearing the words of proposal spoken by the messenger, the beauty said: 'I am a chaste married woman. How can I enter into this arrangement that defiles my chastity? Because:

> One who is expert at running the home,
> bears children,
> loves her husband like her life,
> and is devoted to him—
> she alone qualifies to be called a wife. (199)

> And she who does not please her husband,
> she is not a wife.

> Because it is only through a husband's pleasure
> that a wife appeases the gods. (200)

That's why I unhesitatingly do whatever my husband commands me to.' The messenger said: 'That's true.' The woman replied: 'Yes, absolutely true.'

The messenger then returned to Tungabala and apprised him of the situation. Tungabala then said: 'I am altogether enamoured by her, how will I live without her?' The messenger then said: 'Her husband will herself hand her over to you!' 'How is that possible?' asked the prince. 'Come on! Strategize! For it has been said:

> Strategy can achieve what valour cannot.
> That's how the jackal killed the elephant in the mud.'
> (201)

The prince asked: 'How's that?' The female messenger started to narrate.

THE NINTH STORY

An elephant called Karpuratilaka lived in the Brahma Forest. Seeing his size, all the jackals of the forest thought: 'If we can kill the elephant through some strategy, his flesh will last us four months.' An old one among the jackals vowed: 'I can certainly kill him through the power of my intellect.' This devious jackal then approached the elephant and ceremoniously bowed before him, saying: 'Oh Lord, please have mercy on me.' The elephant asked: 'Who are you and from where have you come?' He replied: 'I am a jackal. All the animals of the forest called a meeting and sent me to you. They have decided that it is not right to live without a king and that you, who possesses all the qualities of an emperor, should be anointed king of this forest. Because:

> One who is brave, righteous, and just
> and well-versed in the ways of the world—
> he alone deserves to rule over this earth. (202)

Further, see:

> First a king should be sought
> and only later a wife and wealth.
> For without a king,
> who will protect home and hearth? (203)
>
> A king, like rain clouds,
> is the very foundation of life.
> People may survive if it does not rain,
> but they cannot if there is no king. (204)
>
> It is only through fear of punishment
> under the reign of the king
> that people perform their duties properly.
> Otherwise, they would all misbehave!
> Just like it is only through fear of punishment
> that a wife accepts even a weak, ill, or impoverished
> husband. (205)

So, please come quickly, lest the auspicious moment of coronation pass.' Saying so, the jackal got up and trotted off, and Karpuratilaka, the elephant, greedy for kingship, ran after him in such a hurry that he fell into heavy slush. He called out: 'Oh friend jackal! What do we do now? I am going to die here in the mud. Come and see.' The jackal laughed and spoke: 'Lord, grab my tail and pull yourself up. And just as you fell for my false words, now face the miserable consequences too. For it is said:

If you escape the company of the wicked,
you will live.
And if you fall for their lot,
you will die!' (206)

Then the trapped elephant was eaten alive by the jackals. And so I say that what strategy can achieve, valour cannot.' On the female messenger's advice, the prince then appointed in his service the son of a merchant named Charudatta and entrusted him with important tasks.

Once again on the advice of the messenger, the prince bathed, and anointed and adorned his body with jewels, and then called for Charudatta. To him he then said: 'I have to perform a month-long ritual to worship Goddess Parvati. Therefore, every night please arrange for me here a young woman of virtue, I will worship her as prescribed.' Charudatta did as he was told and would then hide to watch what the prince was actually going to do with the women. And every night Tungbala would, from a respectful distance, worship the young women, gift them clothes and ornaments, and then send them home escorted by a guard. Charudatta believed what he saw and, driven by greed for the gifts bestowed on the women, brought his own wife, Lavanyavati, to the palace one night. Seeing the object of his ardour before him, Tungbala embraced her tightly and, taking her to the bed, dallied with her. Seeing this, the merchant's son fell into grief. 'And so will you,' said Hiranyaka, finishing his story.

However, not paying heed to Hiranyaka's words of caution, Manthara, the tortoise, beset with anxiety, abandoned his lake and set off. Fearing that the worst may befall him, Hiranyaka and the others also followed Manthara out of care and affection for him.

On the way, a hunter spotted the tortoise crawling on the

ground. He grabbed him and his bow and set off for his home to quench his thirst and hunger. The deer, crow, and mouse followed, bemoaning the turn of events. Hiranyaka lamented:

> 'Even before I can get over one sorrow
> which seems endless like the sea,
> another sorrow shows up.
> Because troubles never arrive alone but in a whole bunch. (207)
>
> It is sheer luck to find a friend
> who is naturally affectionate
> and does not forsake his friendship
> even when calamities strike. (208)
>
> The faith one can have in such a friend
> is not to be had
> even in one's mother, wife, brother, or son. (209)

What bad luck! For:

> All the joys and sorrows of this birth and the last,
> I have witnessed them all here and now! (210)

Or maybe this is just how things are:

> The body holds the seeds of its own destruction.
> Possessions are what bring on calamities.
> Union is followed by separation.
> Everything is fleeting!' (211)

He fell quiet and then again began to think:

> 'A saviour in distress,
> a source of love and trust—
> who created this wondrous thing called a friend? (212)

> A sight for sore eyes, balm to the soul,
> constant companion through good and evil times—
> such a friend is rare.
> Hangers-on in times of prosperity
> are many
> but it is adversity that is the true test of friends.' (213)

Greatly grieving thus, Hiranyaka said to Chitranga, the deer, and Laghupatnaka, the crow: 'You have to rescue Manthara before the hunter exits the forest.' They asked him how. Hiranyaka said: 'Chitranga, go play dead near the water and Laghupatnaka, sit atop him and pretend to peck at the body. The hunter is bound to drop the tortoise in favour of deer flesh and rush over. I will then cut through Manthara's ropes, and when the hunter approaches you, get up and run!'

Chitranga and Laghupatnaka quickly went and did what they were told. The hunter, who had gone to the edge of the lake for a drink of water, sighted the deer in that state under the tree. Elated, he took out a knife and advanced towards it. Hiranyaka seized his chance and helped his friend, the tortoise, out of his shackles. The tortoise jumped straight into the lake. And the deer got up and sprinted as the hunter approached. Bemused, the hunter returned to his spot, only to find the tortoise missing too! He then thought 'I deserve this, since I didn't think things through. Because:

> They who give up the certain
> for the uncertain
> lose out on both.' (214)

Cursing his luck, he returned home disappointed. Manthara and the others too safely went home and lived happily.

◆

The royal princes of Pataliputra then addressed Vishnusharma joyously: 'We are delighted to have heard all this! Our purpose is achieved.' Vishnusharma replied: 'Indeed it is! And may the following too happen:

> May good people find good friends.
> May citizens obtain prosperity.
> May righteous kings forever protect the earth.
> May your knowledge of conduct please the learned
> like a young beauty pleases the heart.
> And may the crescent-bearing God
> Lord Shiva protect the people.' (215)

Here ends the first collection of stories in the *Hitopadesha* called Winning Friends.

BOOK TWO

Losing Friends

Now the princes said: 'Oh noble one! We have heard the section on Winning Friends. Now we want to know all about when friends are lost.' Vishnusharma said: 'Okay, so listen. This is the first verse of this section:

> The lion and the bull
> had become fast friends in the forest.
> The mean and greedy jackal
> tore them apart.' (1)

'How did that happen?' asked the princes. Vishnusharma then began to narrate.

THE FIRST STORY

There is a city named Suvarnagiri on the Dakshinapatha, the Great Southern Route. There lived a merchant named Vardhamana. He owned great riches but, seeing his wealthier friends and relatives, he wanted to earn more. Because:

> Our self-esteem rises when we see our inferiors
> and falls when we see our superiors!
> Before the latter, everyone thinks they are beggarly! (2)

What's more:

> A rich man is venerated
> even if he be a sinner
> while a poor man, even from a pious family,
> reaps insults. (3)

> Just like a young woman does not love
> an old husband,
> so too Lakshmi, the goddess of fortune,
> does not favour the lazy, the fatalist, the coward,
> and those who do not endeavour. (4)
>
> Indeed sloth, debility, complacence, cowardice,
> excessive attachment to a woman,
> and to one's place of origin—
> these six are the enemies of greatness. (5)

Because:

> He who considers himself well-off
> despite having limited resources
> even God considers him a done deal!
> And does not give him more. (6)
>
> May no woman give birth
> to one who lacks zest, joy, and courage,
> and makes life easy for his enemies thereby. (7)

As it has been said:

> Seek wealth that you do not possess.
> Protect wealth that you do.
> Increase it by investments in business, etc.
> And then donate it to good causes. (8)

Because the thirst for profit inevitably attracts wealth. And unprotected wealth is inevitably lost. And if you don't increase your assets, they, like kohl from the eyes, eventually deplete and vanish. But if you don't enjoy and use your wealth at all, it is absolutely worthless.

It has been said:

BOOK TWO: LOSING FRIENDS

> What good is wealth that is neither consumed nor donated?
> What use is power that does not harass one's enemies?
> What is gained from the scriptures if unaccompanied by righteous actions?
> And what is the point of the soul that has not conquered its sense-organs? (9)

> Seeing how kohl gradually decreases
> and an anthill slowly builds up,
> make every day count—
> in studies, piety, and in trade. (10)

Because:

> Just as water, drop by drop, eventually fills up the pitcher,
> so too do knowledge, wealth, and piety
> accumulate
> bit by steady bit. (11)

> He whose life passes without enjoyment or charity,
> he is alive only in name.
> Like the bellow of a blacksmith
> breathes air but is not alive. (12)

Ruminating in this way, Vardhamana loaded his wares on the back of two bullocks, Nandaka and Sanjeevaka, and set off for trade towards the land of Kashmir. For:

> What is too great a burden for one who is strong?
> What is too far a distance for one who is enterprising?
> What is an alien place for one who is educated?
> And who is a stranger for one who speaks sweetly? (13)

Proceeding in this fashion, all of a sudden, deep within the

Sudurga Forest, Sanjeevaka broke his knee and collapsed to the ground. Seeing him Vardhamana started to worry thus:

> No matter how clever a merchant
> and how hard he tries
> to ply his business here and there,
> success comes only if God so wills it. (14)

> But, self-defeating worries are deplorable.
> Abandoning doubt, one should
> keep persevering for success. (15)

Resolving thus, Vardhamana abandoned the poor bull Sanjeevaka there and went to a nearby town called Dharmapur and bought a big new bull. Yoking it to his goods, he then resumed his journey. Meanwhile, Sanjeevaka painfully hauled himself up on his remaining three legs.

For:

> When destined to live,
> those drowning in the ocean,
> or falling off a mountain,
> or bitten by a snake,
> preserve the will to life. (16)

> When one's time has not yet come
> one will survive even though shot by a hundred arrows.
> But when it is time to die,
> even a blade of grass can pierce the heart. (17)

> If protected by destiny, even the defenceless will endure.
> But if destined to die, even the well-guarded will be destroyed.
> Just as a helpless creature in the forest may survive
> but one nursed in the safe confines of a home may not. (18)

After many days had passed, Sanjeevaka, grazing at will, recouped his strength and bellowed loudly. In the same forest there lived a lion named Pingala who had established his reign by sheer might. As they say:

> Deer hardly anoint the lion king!
> He himself seizes control
> through his prowess
> and then calls himself their leader. (19)

Pingala one day approached the Yamuna River for a drink of water. There he heard the thunderous bellow of Sanjeevaka. Terrified, he ran away without a sip and, once safely back at his lair, sat dazed, quietly wondering what on earth that sound was. That is how the sons of his minister, two jackals by the name of Damanaka and Karataka, found him.

Seeing his stunned condition, Damanaka said to Karataka: 'Brother, how come the Lord is so afraid that though thirsty he shunned a drink of water and is sitting here without a word?' Karataka replied: 'Brother Damanaka, in my opinion, we should not serve him any further. So even if he is in trouble, what do we care? We have been humiliated by this king for ages and without any fault either.

> Hoping to get rich by the master's favour
> see what servitors have done!
> The fools have squandered
> all their independence! (20)

> Slaves, braving the cold, heat, and other elements
> suffer greatly.
> Whereas a smart person can succeed
> on a fraction
> of their labour and suffering. (21)

Independence is the greatest gift of life.
Those who are dependent on others—
are they even alive? (22)

"Come here!" "Go there!" "Sit!" "Stand!"
"Speak up!" "Quiet now!"
This is how the rich toy
with the needy hopefuls in their service. (23)

And just as a prostitute decks up
for the sake of others
so too these fools, for the sake of money,
have spruced up and sold their souls to others. (24)

They pride themselves if their master
even so much as notices them.
Never mind if the same fickle glance
rests also on the master's waste matter! (25)

Servants can never seem to get it right!
If they are quiet, they are called stupid.
If they speak up, they are called talkative.
If they are tolerant, they are called cowards.
If they can't bear it, they are called low-born.
If they stand close, they are called insolent.
And if they stand afar, they are told they are not bold!
The duty of servants is an impossible enigma
that even spiritual adepts cannot fathom! (26)

Only a servant can be so foolish
that to rise high, he bends low;
to live, he gives up life;
and to be happy, he embraces sorrows!' (27)

Damanaka, however, said: 'Hey, buddy, don't even think such things! Because:

> Why shouldn't one serve a master
> who, pleased with our service,
> quickly fulfils our ardent wishes? (28)

> And, but for being in service,
> how else would we ever
> get to enjoy the pomp and power
> of the royal staff and umbrella
> and an army of horses and elephants?' (29)

Karataka said: 'Even so, why should we be bothered about what troubles the king? If one does not mind one's own business, one may lose everything. See!

> They who interfere
> in what is not their concern
> lose their lives, just like the monkey
> who tried to pull out the nail.' (30)

Damanaka asked: 'What happened?' Karataka began to narrate.

THE SECOND STORY

In the land of Magadha, near the Dharma Forest, a scribe by the name of Shubhadatta began to build a monastery. There the carpenter had sawed a log of wood halfway through and then driven a wedge in to keep the cleft open. A troop of big monkeys was playing nearby. As if driven by fate, one of them sat on the log and grabbed the wedge. His testicles meanwhile hung over the cleft. As the monkey excitedly tugged this way and that and finally uprooted the wedge, the cleft snapped shut and his testicles were crushed, killing him. 'This is why I say don't meddle with things that are no concern of yours,' said Karataka.

'Even so,' said Damanaka, 'a servitor should always look out for his master's concerns.' But Karataka rejoined: 'Let the prime minister do it then, for he is in charge of all affairs. A servitor should never get into business that belongs to another. See:

> With his master's interests at heart
> he who discusses the jurisdiction of another
> is killed
> just like the donkey who was beaten to death
> for braying.' (31)

Damanaka asked: 'How did that happen?' So Karataka started to narrate.

THE THIRD STORY

There lived in Banaras a washerman by the name of Karpurapataka. One night he dallied for long with his young wife and then, clasping her to himself, fell asleep. Just then a thief entered his compound. There sat the washerman's donkey and his dog. The donkey said to the dog: 'Hey, isn't it your job to bark and warn the master about the thief?' The dog replied: 'Don't you bother with my job! Moreover, the master takes me and my services for granted and does not even feed me well any more. Indeed, masters remember their servants only when calamity strikes.'

The donkey said:

> 'Listen, you brute!
> He who makes demands in the hour of need

is a despicable servant
and, indeed, a despicable friend.' (32)

The dog said:

'Well, he who is kind to his servants
only in his hour of need,
he is a despicable master! (33)

Because:

There are some things that must be done oneself
and brook no delegation.
These include looking after dependents and masters,
performing rituals, and begetting a child!' (34)

Then the donkey got annoyed and said: 'You crook! You are a terrible person for abandoning the master's duty in a crisis. Fine! I will do whatever it takes to ensure the master wakes. Because:

One must serve the master
in every way possible
just as one must pursue heaven
in the life after death.' (35)

Having spoken in this way, the good donkey began to bray like crazy! The washerman was rudely awoken and, annoyed, came out and began beating the donkey with a stick, killing him eventually.

'This is why I said don't meddle in the affairs of others,' said Karataka, 'Our job is just to stake out prey, speak only of that.' Then after thinking for a minute he continued: 'But today there is no point discussing even that. Because there is plenty left over from our meal yesterday.'

Damanaka was annoyed: 'Do you serve the king only to

fill your stomach? This is wrong! Because:

> The clever serve the king
> for the benefit of their friends
> and the destruction of their enemies.
> Filling the stomach is hardly extraordinary.
> Who doesn't do that? (36)
>
> Who doesn't live just for oneself?
> But they who work
> for the good of Brahmins, friends, and relatives,
> their lives are truly blessed. (37)
>
> He whose life helps support
> the lives of many others,
> he has lived in truth.
> All others are like crows
> who with their beaks
> fill only their own bellies. (38)
>
> Look, some can be bought into slavery for a few pennies
> while others may sell their service for a lakh.
> But some are not for sale at all! (39)

What's more:

> When all humans are equal
> servitude of another is repugnant.
> What to speak of those servants
> who are low down the pecking order?
> Their lives are wretched! (40)
>
> For just as no two horses, elephants, metals, wood,
> stones, cloths, or kinds of water are alike,
> no two humans are of the same rank either. (41)

> A dog is content with a bare bone
> bereft of any flesh or sinew
> even though it does not sate his hunger.
> But a lion will forego a dead jackal
> and prefer to bring down an elephant to eat.
> So, all creatures set goals
> befitting their abilities and stature. (42)

Further, mark the difference between master and servant:

> A dog wags at the one who throws him crumbs,
> rolls at his feet,
> and shows his belly in submission.
> But a mighty elephant looks but calmly at his owner
> and eats only when he is fussed over. (43)

> Indeed, the wise regard his life a success
> who, though lives but for a short while,
> wins fame for his learning and valour.
> Others are no better than the crow
> who lives long but does precious more than eat. (44)

> And in the same way
> what is the point of the life of one
> who shows no kindness to children, teachers,
> servitors, and needy friends?
> Indeed, even the crow lives long
> and does little more than eat. (45)

> Pray, what is the difference
> between an animal
> and a human being
> who is stubborn and unlearned
> and lives only to eat?' (46)

Karataka then said: 'We are in any case mere subordinates. Why should we be bothered by what's going on with the king?' Damanaka replied: 'It takes no time to rise up the order or fall. Because:

> None is born superior or inferior
> in this world.
> It is through one's efforts alone that one
> rises or falls in stature. (47)
>
> In fact, it is easier to be tempted by evil
> than to cultivate virtue
> just as it is easier to toss a rock down a hillside
> than to roll it to the top of the hill. (48)
>
> It is through one's own actions
> that one can ascend or descend in life.
> Like one who builds a palace, ascending to the top,
> or digs a well, descending to its bottom. (49)

So, my dear, it is only appropriate that each one's position depends on their efforts.' Karataka said: 'So what do you say we do?' Damanaka replied: 'Our master Pingala has had a fright somewhere for some reason.' Karataka asked: 'Do you know the reason?' Damanaka said: 'What's there not to know? It has been said:

> Even animals can understand the obvious message
> like a horse or elephant can follow the goad.
> Clever people, on the other hand,
> can divine the truth by deduction,
> for to gauge the secrets of others
> is the work of true intelligence! (50)

> One can tell the inner workings of the mind
> from a person's features, gestures,
> his gait, his words,
> and the flickering changes in his eyes and face. (51)

So let me exploit the master's fright to win him over by the power of my intellect. Because:

> The wise know how to adapt their speech
> to the occasion,
> their affection to the friend,
> and their anger to the limits of their prowess.' (52)

But Karataka piped up: 'No way! You don't know how to serve a king! See:

> One who rushes in uninvited,
> speaks unasked,
> and considers himself the king's best friend
> is a fool!' (53)

Damanaka retorted: 'Hey, I do know how to serve! Look:

> Nothing is attractive or repulsive per se.
> It all depends on what is of interest to whom. (54)

> An intelligent person should gauge
> what the other needs
> and, acting accordingly,
> proceed to win him over. (55)

> One should therefore enter saying,
> "Lord! Command me to do your bidding!",
> and then do one's best to follow through. (56)

> In fact, every king must have in his service
> a person with few needs,

great patience and wisdom,
and who, like his shadow,
acts instantly on command.' (57)

Karataka said: 'What if you approach him at a bad time and the master insults you?' Damanaka replied: 'Even at that risk, a servitor should definitely approach the master. Because:

Only a coward shuns a task
for fear of being faulted.
Do we give up food
for fear of indigestion? (58)

And further, look:

A king favours the man who is around him
even if he is lowly, ignorant, or unworthy.
In fact, a king, a woman, and a creeper
all cling to whoever is near them!' (59)

Karataka then said: 'Okay, what will you say when you go there?' So Damanaka said: 'I will first try to make out whether the master is pleased or displeased with me.' 'And how can one know that, what are the signs?' asked Karataka. Damanaka said: 'Well, listen:

These are the signs of a well-disposed master:
if he looks at you with anticipation, if he smiles
and asks after your well-being,
if he praises you behind your back,
and calls you a favourite. (60)

And if he is indulgent even when you don't serve,
and invokes your virtues even when you have erred,
and if he gives you gifts along with sweet words,

such a master is pleased with you. (61)

But if he again and again postpones
any favour you need
and raises your hopes only to shatter them
these are all signs
of a master displeased with you. (62)

So, looking out for these signs, I will proceed to do what it takes to win him over. Because:

The intelligent can foresee both
failures resulting from bad tactics
and successes resulting from smart solutions.' (63)

Karataka butted in: 'Even so, without landing a good opportunity, you cannot accomplish anything. Because:

Even Lord Brihaspati, the creator,
if speaking out of context,
will be decried and disgraced.' (64)

Damanaka said: 'Listen, don't worry. I won't be speaking out of turn or context. Because:

A well-meaning servant
must by all means speak up
when there is a crisis looming,
or the master is going astray,
or the proper time for action is passing. (65)

And if I didn't so counsel, I wouldn't deserve to be a minister. Because:

One must preserve and enhance
the qualities by which we earn a living
and the praise of the good in this world. (66)

Therefore, my good man, let me now set off.' Karataka replied: 'Very well. May success abide with you. And may you achieve what you are setting out to do.' Then Damanaka gingerly approached Pingala.

The king courteously called him in. Damanaka prostrated before the king in obeisance and then took a seat. The king spoke: 'I am seeing you after a long time.' Damanaka replied: 'Even though the master may have no use for him, a follower must call on the master when the time comes. That's why I have come. Further, oh king:

> Even a straw is needed by kings
> to scratch an itch in the ear
> or scrape the plaque off their teeth.
> How much more so the need
> for a living, breathing person? (67)

And in case you think I may have lost my mental faculties from long years of being overlooked for service, you should have no such apprehensions. Because:

> Just as fire always billows upwards
> even if it is lit down below,
> so too the intelligence of a neglected but patient man
> must never be doubted. (68)

And this is why the master must always have a discriminating intellect. Because:

> It is possible that jewels may languish on the feet
> while beads of glass adorn the head.
> Each, however, stays what it is: a jewel is a jewel,
> glass is merely glass. (69)

And if the king treats alike
the worthy and the worthless
then the morale of the hard-working, capable person
is destroyed. (70)

Oh king, there are three kinds of people:
the good, the no good, and the mediocre.
They should be entrusted with tasks too
of different kinds accordingly. (71)

For, just like ornaments,
followers too must be placed
in deserving positions.
A crown is not worn on the feet
and an anklet cannot adorn the head. (72)

Further, if a jewel that behoves gold ornaments
is set in ornaments of lead,
it ceases to shine or tinkle
and brings disgrace to its jeweller. (73)

Likewise, if glass is used to craft the crown
while gems are set in ornaments for the feet
none will blame the precious stones for their position;
it is the jeweller's folly that will be called out. (74)

See, my lord, the king who can gauge
which of his servitors
is intelligent, devoted, brave, or treacherous—
such an astute king is never wanting for followers. (75)

For it has been said: horses, arms, books of high learning,
musical instruments, speech, and all men and women
acquire their worth or lack of it
depending on whether they are wielded by

a deserving person or an undeserving one. (76)

And what is the point of having
an incompetent loyal or a disloyal adept?
So, oh king, you should not ignore a man like me
who is both devoted and capable. (77)

When a person is respected by the king
the whole world respects him
whereas one insulted by the king
is scoffed at by everyone. (78)

And when a king insults his inner circle,
they lose their minds.
And other wise men also, apprehending humiliation,
do not approach the king's service.
And when a kingdom lacks wise counsellors,
governance and policy deteriorate,
which in turn destroys the whole world. (79)

A man of intellect should pay heed to good advice
even from a child.
For doesn't a lamp also give light
when the sun does not emerge?' (80)

Then Pingala, the lion, spoke: 'Dear Damanaka, what is this? Did some villain instigate you, my own prime minister's son, to avoid coming here for so long? Anyway, tell me now, what it is you seek.' Damanaka replied: 'Oh king, I will ask you a question, do tell. Why are you sitting here all frightened with your thirst still unquenched?' Pingala answered: 'Good question. But there's nobody reliable here to reveal this secret to. But I guess it's just you and me here so I can speak. An extraordinary new creature has taken up residence in this jungle and we will have to vacate this place soon. That's what is worrying me. He makes a terrible bellow as well, which tells me he must be of gigantic proportions and strength.' Damanaka said: 'Oh king, this is indeed a cause for fear. I have also heard that terrific sound. But only a bad minister will advise flight before a fight. And:

> It is only in an adversity
> that a person
> knows the true worth
> of his friends, wife, and followers.' (81)

The lion said: 'Oh well-wisher, I am truly in a fearful bind.' Damanaka thought: 'Obviously! Why else would you talk about forfeiting the pleasures of kingship and going off elsewhere?' Aloud he said: 'You have no reason to fear as long as I am alive. But do entrust Karataka and others as well, for many heads are better than one in a crisis.' In response, the king feted both Damanaka and Karataka with gifts. The two swore to resolve the crisis and then they were off. On the way, Karataka said to Damanaka: 'Hey, pal, we should have first contemplated whether this problem is even resolvable before vowing to resolve it and accepting all these gifts for the same. Without getting the job done, one should never accept gifts from anyone, least of all the king. See:

> When pleased, he is the bestower of fortune.
> When valorous, he is the bestower of victory.
> But when angered, he is the bestower of death!
> Even in infancy thus a king
> should never be regarded a mere mortal.
> He is God incarnate!' (82–83)

Damanaka laughed and said: 'Just relax! I already know the problem and its cause. It is merely a bull's bellow. And the bull is an animal of prey for us, let alone for the lion!' Karataka asked: 'But if that's the case, why didn't you say so and put an end to the master's fear there and then?' Damanaka replied: 'If I had done that, would we have received all these beautiful clothes and jewels? Moreover:

> A servant must ensure that the master
> is never free from needing his services.
> A servant who fails to be needed is killed
> like Dadhikarna, the cat.' (84)

Karataka asked: 'What happened there?' Damanaka began to narrate.

THE FOURTH STORY

On the great Uttarapatha, the Northern Route, there once lived atop Mount Arbudashikhara, a mighty lion by the name of Durdanta. When he slept inside his cave atop that hill, a mouse routinely nibbled on his mane. Infuriated to find his hair chewed up, and the mouse safely back inside his burrow, the lion got thinking:

> 'When the enemy is puny
> and invincible by valour,
> it is best to beat him by a warrior
> matching his dimensions. (85)

Having so determined, he went to the village nearby and got himself a cat named Dadhikarna. Feeding him meat, he kept him as a pet inside his cave. As expected, the mouse stopped emerging from his burrow for fear of the cat, and the lion could now sleep peacefully, with no risk of his mane being nibbled.

If he ever heard squeaks from the mouse, he fed his cat with renewed attention.

Now once, desperate for food, when the mouse risked an outing from his hole, the cat easily caught and killed it. As a result, the lion did not see the mouse around or hear its squeaks for a long time and, knowing the cat to be of little use now, stopped bothering to feed it. Poor Dadhikarna soon weakened and died from starvation. This is why I say a master should never be freed from needing your services.'

Having made the point, Damanaka along with Karataka went to meet Sanjeevaka, the bull. Once there, Karataka sat down with a show of arrogance, while Damanaka went up to Sanjeevaka and said: 'Oh bull, I have been appointed by King Pingala to guard the forest. Commander-in-chief Karataka sitting there hereby commands you to come with us immediately or flee the forest, otherwise there will be hell to pay. Better listen, for the master, if annoyed, may wreak havoc.' Hearing this, Sanjeevaka went along with him.

> Disobeying a royal order,
> insulting a Brahmin,
> and allowing a woman her separate bed:
> these are akin to suicide! (86)

Not conversant with the customs of the land, Sanjeevaka hesitantly approached Karataka and bowed before him. As it has been said:

> Brains are mightier than brawn!
> This is the only reason why
> mighty elephants can be reduced
> to dire straits of captivity
> by humans. (87)

Sanjeevaka then spoke somewhat doubtfully: 'Oh commander-in-chief, please tell me what it is I am to do.' Karataka replied: 'Oh bull, if you stay in this forest, you must prostrate before the king and salute him.' Sanjeevaka said: 'Assure me my safety and I will comply.' Karataka replied: 'Listen, stop having these doubts!

> Lord Krishna did not so much as reply
> when the king of Chedi, Shishupala,
> kept abusing him.
> Because a lion roars in reply to thunder,
> not to the shrieks of a hyena! (88)

> And, a storm does not uproot
> tiny, bent over leaves of grass,
> only the tall and mighty oak trees.
> Because the high and mighty show their might,
> only those like them are uprooted.' (89)

Then they all set off and as Pingala's abode neared, they left Sanjeevaka at a bit of a distance and approached the lion. The lion looked respectfully at them and the two bowed and took their seats. Pingala asked: 'Did you see it?' Damanaka replied: 'Oh king, we did. And it is just as you had feared: Huge! It wants to meet you and is very strong, so please sit tight and alert. However, one should not take fright from mere sound. It has been said:

> Do not fear a sound without getting to the root of it.
> It is from detecting the cause of the sound
> that the bawd won respect. (90)

The king said: 'What was that all about?' So Damanaka began to narrate.

THE FIFTH STORY

There was a town called Brahmapura on the Shriparvata Mountain. It was said that a demon by the name of Ghantakarna (Bell-ears) lived on the upper reaches of that hill. One day a robber who had stolen a bell and was running away was captured and killed by a tiger. The bell that had fallen from his hand was picked up by a bunch of monkeys nearby. They would shake and sound the bell repeatedly. The townspeople added two and two and surmised that the demon had eaten the robber and was ringing the bell in glee! In terror, they turned on their heels and ran away from the town.

Only a procuress named Karala gave pause and observed that the bell seemed to ring without any occasion. She then wondered if it was the monkeys who were ringing it. On checking and confirming that that was indeed the case, she came up with a plan. She went and told the king of Brahmapura that if he spared some wealth and resources, she could get the better of the demon! The king promptly gave her what she wanted. She then organized an elaborate puja of Lord Ganesh and other gods, and later, purchasing lots of fruit that monkeys like, scattered them all over the forest. The simians duly dropped the bell and went for the fruit! The procuress then returned to town with that bell and was greatly feted and respected for her 'feat'! This is why I say do not be afraid of a mere sound.

Speaking thus, Damanaka brought Sanjeevaka over and introduced him to the lion. The bull thereafter settled down there and lived happily.

When some time had elapsed, Pingala's brother, Stabhdhakarna, arrived. Pingala received him warmly and after settling him in, began to leave to hunt them a meal. At this, Sanjeevaka queried: 'Oh king, where is all the meat from the deer you killed?' Pingala replied: 'No idea, Damanaka and Karataka would know.' 'Then call them and find out if the meat is around or not.' Pingala gave it some thought and said that no meat was left. Sanjeevaka exclaimed: 'How on earth did the two of them wipe out so much meat?' The king replied: 'They ate some, distributed some, and threw away the rest, I guess. This has become routine around here.' 'Why do they behave like this behind your back, oh king?' asked Sanjeevaka. 'This is wrong! For it has been said:

> Except for solving a crisis,
> servants must not take any action
> without the master's express consent. (91)

> And, oh king, a minister should be like a jar of holy water—
> expending little and conserving a lot.
> Only a fool does not value time
> and a beggar every paisa. (92)

> Only a minister who saves up wealth bit by bit
> is worth his salt.
> For a king's vital essence lies in his treasury
> and not merely in his body. (93)

> And without wealth, a man does not acquire respect
> no matter how good his lineage or conduct.
> For even his own wife deserts a pauper;
> why won't all others then? (94)

And among the faults in a king are:

> Overspending wealth, disinterest in wealth,
> unjustly acquired or grabbed wealth,
> and not supervising his wealth. (95)

> Above all, exhausting one's accumulated wealth
> in a mindless hurry
> reduces even the lord of wealth
> to a pauper before long.' (96)

Stabhdhakarna then spoke up: 'Listen, brother. These two fellows Damanaka and Karataka have been ripping us off for a long time. They are fit only for battle, not to oversee the treasury. For such a sensitive task, I have heard the following:

> A Brahmin, a Kshatriya, and a relative
> should never be put in positions of authority.
> The Brahmin will take a long time to hand over wealth
> even when requested by the king.
> The Kshatriya if put in charge of the treasury
> will draw his sword in rebellion soon after.
> And a relative, emboldened by familiarity with the king,
> will rob all the wealth. (97–98)

> Further, an old hand given the job
> will steal with impunity
> and, disobeying the king,
> act in unfettered ways. (99)

> A benefactor if entrusted with the position
> will go on about the obligation
> he has done the king
> and hide his faults and errors behind that. (100)

> A childhood friend appointed as minister
> knows inside out the king's ways
> and as such behaves like a king himself,
> despising the king out of familiarity. (101)

Oh king, an officer who acts a well-wisher
but is a villain in reality
ends up destroying everything.
Shakuni, Duryodhana's aide,
and Shaktara, Mahananda's minister,
are two prime examples. (102)

Ministers spoilt on wealth
ultimately betray the king
because, as the wise have said,
pomp and pelf corrupt the conscience. (103)

In fact, a minister's faults include:
taking over wealth, laundering it,
asking for more repeatedly,
callous or brainless at work,
and given over to debauchery. (104)

Exhausting the king's assets, spying on the king,
bribing him based on his weaknesses,
and being lackadaisical towards his duties—
these are also a minister's faults. (105)

Like a putrid boil, ministers
do not cough up the king's money
unless they are pressed hard to do so. (106)

Oh king, you must frequently inspect
the assets of all your officers.
For a wet towel wrung just once
does not yield all the absorbed water, does it? (107)

Please implement all this counsel at appropriate occasions.' The lion spoke: 'Well, this is all true, but these fellows are not going to listen.' Stabhdhakarna then said: 'This is all so wrong! Because:

> A king must not forgive those
> who disobey him
> even if they are his own sons.
> What else distinguishes a real king
> from a mere portrait of him? (108)

> A kingdom with unwise minsters is destroyed
> just like a lazybones's reputation, a fickle man's friendship,
> a debaucher's family, a greedy man's conscience,
> a gambler's education, and a miser's joy of life. (109)

> A king, like a father, must protect his subjects
> from thieves and enemies
> but also from his own favourites and other officers
> and, indeed, from his own avarice. (110)

Brother, please do heed what I say, for I too have run a kingdom. You should appoint this Sanjeevaka here, a grass eater, in charge of your food resources.' Doing as he was advised by his brother, Pingala let go all his relatives from service and then lived happily and in great friendship with Sanjeevaka for a long time. But finding their allowances slashed, Karataka and Damanaka began to worry. Damanaka said: 'Buddy, what do we do now? We are ourselves responsible for what has happened, we can't even complain!

> Indeed, I for touching Svarnalekha (the golden line),
> the procuress for tying herself up,
> and the merchant for coveting the jewel:
> we are all responsible for our own problems!' (111)

Karataka wondered what that was all about and so Damanaka began to narrate.

THE SIXTH STORY

In the city of Kanchanapura, there lived a brave king, Vikrama by name. Once his law officer was taking a convicted barber for execution when an ascetic passing by, named Kandarpaketu, called out: 'He does not deserve to die!' So saying, he quickly hid the barber inside his cloak. The king's officer asked in astonishment what he meant. The ascetic replied: 'I for touching the golden line, the procuress for tying herself up, and the merchant for coveting the jewel: we are all responsible for our own problems!' The king's men pressed further, so the ascetic started to narrate:

'I, Kandarpaketu, am the son of the king of Sri Lanka, Jimutaketu. Once when I was sitting in a beautiful leisure garden, I heard a seafarer say that on the fourteenth day of the lunar fortnight, a wish-fulfilling tree blooms right there in the middle of the ocean. And under that wondrous tree, atop a bed all aglitter with emeralds and rubies, there appears a gorgeous and bejewelled nymph, resembling the goddess of fortune herself and playing a lute. On hearing this, I set off for that spot with the seaman on his boat. On reaching, sure enough, we saw the nymph atop a half-submerged bed. Drawn in by her allure, I dove into the waters and when I emerged, I had reached the city of Kanakapura, the Golden City, and beheld there in a golden palace the same girl on her jewelled bed served by celestial maids. She too saw me and sent one of her friends to have me respectfully called over.

I seized my chance and asked her friend all about the girl. I learnt that she, Ratnamanjari by name, was the daughter of the king of apsaras, Kandarpakeli. And she had taken a vow that regardless of her father's consent, she would marry the person who succeeded in reaching the Golden City and set eyes on her.

The friend then implored me that I was the one who ought to marry Ratnamanjari. I did just that! And then spent my days in a love dalliance in that palace.

Then one day Ratnamanjari told me that I could enjoy myself as much as I wanted while living there, but I should never, even by mistake, touch a golden sketch of an apsara, Svarnalekha, that sat in the palace. My curiosity, however, got the better of me one day and I did the unthinkable. The painted figure came alive at my touch and gave me such a royal kick that I was thrown back to my own kingdom!

Sorrowful beyond words, I became an ascetic and roamed the world, ending up here in this town. Once, I took shelter at the house of a cowherd. That evening, the cowherd, on returning from the liquor shop where he had met his friends, caught sight of his wife in secret conversation with a procuress. He beat up his wife and, tying her to a pillar, went off to bed. Later that night, the same procuress sent her daughter to the wife with the message that her secret lover, smitten by Cupid's arrows, was yearning desperately for her. 'Seeing him in that forlorn state, I have come here to set you free and take your place tied to the pillar. Go, satisfy him, and return quickly.' In the meantime the cowherd woke, and hearing snatches of this conversation, said to the woman: 'Come! Let me despatch you to your lover, you sinful woman!' The messenger kept quiet, which infuriated the man even more. 'So arrogant that you won't even answer me?' Picking up a knife, he chopped off her nose, and then went promptly back to bed!

By and by, when the cowherd's wife returned, she saw what had happened to the messenger. She took her place while the procuress' daughter picked up her severed nose and went home. There, the next morning, her father-in-law, a barber, asked her for his shaving kit. She, however, only put out his shaving blade.

Annoyed, the barber threw the blade back inside the house. At this, the procuress' daughter seized the opportunity to raise a hue and cry that the barber had chopped off her nose for no fault of hers. And she took him away to the law officer. And at the cowherd's house, the cowherd asked his wife again about her affair but she indignantly replied: 'Oh, you sinner! Who dare disfigure a woman as chaste as me? My faultless conduct is known even to the gods. Because:

> The sun, the moon, the wind, and the fire,
> the heavens, the earth, the waters, and the heart,
> the day, the night, the dusk, and death itself
> all know the conduct of people. (112)

If my purity is supreme, and I have not known a man other than you, nor seen another man even in my dreams, then may my purity restore my cut nose. I can reduce you to ashes in a trice, but you are my husband and I care for what people will say. So, look! Look at my face!' The cowherd lit a lamp and, seeing her face intact, fell at her feet in astonishment, saying: 'I am the luckiest man to have such a chaste and devoted wife!'

Then Kandarpaketu continued to tell the third tale of the merchant. A merchant left his home on travels and after twelve years arrived at a town near Malyachalaka. There he slept with a prostitute. Outside the prostitute's door was a wooden image of a ghoul with a priceless gem embedded in its head. The covetous merchant got up at night and tried to extract the gem. Suddenly, the wooden puppet stretched out its arms and caught him. He cried out. The prostitute came running and told the merchant to hand over to the ghoul all his own jewels gathered from Malaya Country or he would never let him go. He did as he was told and then, reduced to penury, the merchant joined me, the ascetic.'

Hearing all this, the king's men sent the law officer to investigate, who promptly had the cowherdess and the procuress exiled from the kingdom, and the barber released and sent home. 'And this is why I say,' said Damanaka, 'that just like touching Svarnalekha etc., this too is our own fault. Who else can we blame!' At this, he paused a moment thinking to himself, and then spoke aloud: 'But just as I brought the lion and the bull together in friendship, I shall also split them up. Because:

> Just like a painter of a landscape
> conjures the illusion of mountains in the background
> and a house and tree in the foreground
> all on the same page,
> so too can a clever person
> make a figment seem real. (113)

And, further:

> They who keep their wits about them
> no matter the magnitude of the task
> can extract themselves from any problem
> just like the cowherdess
> who extracted herself from two lovers! (114)

Karataka asked what that was about. So Damanaka began to narrate.

THE SEVENTH STORY

There lived in the city of Dvarawati, the wife of a cowherd, who was of loose morals. She was having an affair with both the city magistrate and his son! After all, it has been said:

> Fire never tires of wood,
> the sea never has enough of rivers,
> death never tires of creatures,
> and women never get enough of men! (115)

> Indeed, it is very difficult for women to be restrained
> by any means: money, respect, straightforwardness,
> devotion, force, or the scriptures. (116)

> Women may yet leave a talented, handsome, young,
> reputable, and sensual husband
> for one bereft of all character and quality. (117)

And further:

> They prefer to lie on the grass with their lovers
> than on a luxurious bed with their husband! (118)

Once she was dallying with the magistrate's son when the magistrate too came by. She hurriedly hid the son in the barn and then proceeded to make love with the magistrate. Soon it was time for her husband to get home, so she told the magistrate to wield a stick in his hand and rush out of the house as if in anger. The cowherd saw him leaving in that state and asked the wife why the man had come to his house. The wife replied that he was chasing his son in anger who had entered their house and hidden himself in a panic. She said the boy suddenly rushed into their house and so she gave him shelter in the barn and saved him from his father's wrath. The wife then proceeded to show the boy to her husband in the barn. This is why it is said:

> Women have twice the appetite of men
> four times their brains
> six times the courage

and eight times their libido! (119)

Anyhow, this is why I said they who retain their wits can rescue themselves from any problem,' concluded Damanaka. Karataka said: 'Hmm, may it turn out so. But how exactly are you going to separate the lion and the bull, they have become fast friends.' Damanaka replied: 'By stratagem! It has been said:

> That which is possible by stratagem
> is not possible even by valour.
> Just like the crow's wife used the gold necklace
> to kill the serpent.' (120)

Karataka again asked: 'How did that happen?' So Damanaka began to narrate.

THE EIGHTH STORY

Once in a tree there lived a pair of crows. Their nestlings were often eaten up by a black snake that lived in the hollow of the tree. When the crow's wife was with child again, she said to her husband: 'Dear, we must leave this tree. The black snake here always kills our babies.

> Remember, death abounds where there is
> a wicked wife, a villainous friend,
> an insolent servant,
> or a house with a resident snake.' (121)

The crow replied: 'Dear, don't worry. I have borne his treachery again and again. But not any more.' His wife asked: 'How will you fight such a powerful foe?' 'Don't have any doubts,' her husband replied, 'because:

> Where there is intelligence,
> there is power.
> Fools have no strength at all.
> See how the arrogant lion was killed by a rabbit.' (122)

The wife asked how and so the crow began to narrate.

THE NINTH STORY

Atop Mount Mandara there lived a lion by the name of Durdanta. He would routinely kill the animals around. Ultimately, all the animals got together and pleaded with him thus: 'Oh lion, why do you kill so many of us all the time? If it pleases you, let us ourselves send you one animal a day for your meal.' The lion replied: 'Sure, if that's what you want.' Ever after he would eat the one animal that was sent to him daily.

Then one day it was the turn of an old rabbit. He thought to himself:

> 'One appeases a killer from fear of death
> in the hope of escaping alive.
> But if death is certain,
> why should I care for this lion? (123)

So let me move at my own sweet pace.' The lion, agitated with hunger, thundered at him when he arrived: 'Why the hell are you so late?' The rabbit replied: 'Oh king, I am not to blame. I was caught by another lion on my way here. I promised I'd return to him just so I could get away and come here to you.'

'Hurry up and show me where that wicked fellow is!' roared Durdanta.

The rabbit promptly took him to a deep well and, telling the lion to see for himself, showed him his own reflection in the water! The enraged lion roared fiercely and jumped right onto the other 'lion', killing himself in the process. 'And this is why I say that where there is intelligence, there is power,' said the crow.

'Okay, I get it. So what do you propose to do now?' said the wife. The crow replied: 'The royal prince comes to bathe in a pond nearby. While he's bathing, pick up his gold necklace from the banks and drop it in the hollow of the tree.' One day when the prince entered the pond for a dip, the crow's wife did as she was told. There followed an uproarious search by the king's men for the missing necklace. Checking in the tree hollow, they found the snake and killed him there and then.

'And this is why I say that which is possible by stratagem is not possible even by valour,' concluded Damanaka. 'Okay, if that's so, please head off. I wish you the best,' said Karataka. Damanaka then went to Pingala and, saluting him, spoke: 'Oh king! I have come upon hearing of something fearful and menacing. Because:

> A well-wisher should always speak up
> in times of crisis, or when the king is going astray,
> or when the right time for action is passing. (124)

And, further:

> A king's job is to enjoy his rule, not to work.
> It is his minister who must bear the blame
> if things go wrong
> in the kingdom. (125)

Which is why, see:

> It is better for a minister to give up his life
> and have his head cut off

than to not report one who
is trying to usurp the king's position.' (126)

Pingala queried: 'What are you trying to say?' Damanaka respectfully replied: 'Lord, this Sanjeevaka seems a worthless fellow to me. I heard him criticizing you for lacking all qualities of a king and stating that he would seize your throne.' Hearing this, Pingala fell silent with fear and disbelief. Damanaka again spoke up: 'Oh king, you doing away with all other ministers and instating him as the be-all and end-all is responsible for what has happened. Because:

If a king and his minister
both prosper equally
the goddess of fortune soon
chooses one over the other! (127)

Moreover:

When a king entrusts all work to one minister alone,
it goes to his head.
Blinded by arrogance, the minister
soon defies the king
wanting to establish his sovereignty
for which he is even ready to murder the king! (128)

And such a wicked minister, like a rotten tooth
and a poisoned meal,
should be uprooted and discarded. (129)

Moreover, a king who relies excessively on one minister
for all his jobs
is lost and incapacitated like the blind
on the minister's death or departure. (130)

Sanjeevaka does as he pleases in all matters. You, oh king, now decide what should be done. You know, in any case, that:

> There is no one who does not
> covet the goddess of wealth.
> Can you think of any man who does not
> ogle at a young and beautiful woman?' (131)

The lion said: 'Oh well-wisher, even if this is the case, Sanjeevaka and I share a very beautiful friendship. See:

> One who is dear to us will always remain dear
> despite their faults.
> Like who isn't still attached to their bodies
> despite all its drawbacks? (132)

> And even if a loved one wrongs us,
> we still love them.
> If fire burns down a temple,
> does it cease to be venerated?' (133)

Damanaka tried again: 'Lord, this is a huge mistake. Because:

> Son, minister, or commoner—
> whoever the king favours in excess,
> the goddess of fortune also gravitates to him. (134)

Listen, oh king:

> However bitter the pill,
> if it is good for you, it should be taken.
> And where there are givers and takers of good advice
> prosperity prevails. (135)

It was also wrong of you to abandon your old followers for this new one. For there can be no greater source of disenchantment and conflict in a kingdom than this.'

The lion said: 'Strange. Why would someone I gave amnesty to and promoted betray me?' Damanaka replied:

> 'Lord, the wicked do not reform
> even if supplicated.
> Just as a dog's tail does not straighten
> even if massaged. (136)
>
> Indeed, even if you oil and fasten a dog's tail with rope
> and leave it for twelve years
> it will still emerge twisted! (137)
>
> Moreover, the wicked are never appeased
> by honour or promotion.
> Even if watered with nectar,
> a poison tree will never yield sweet fruit. (138)

That's why I say:

> One should speak up in the interests of those
> who you never want to see lose in life.
> This is the duty of the good.
> To do otherwise is evil. (139)

And it has been said:

> The one who saves us from disaster
> is the one who truly loves us.
> Like the action that is pure
> is the only true action.
> The woman who is obedient
> is the true woman.
> The one who the virtuous praise
> is the truly intelligent.

> The wealth that does not breed contempt
> is the true wealth.
> The one who is bereft of desires
> is truly happy.
> The one who is devoid of deceit
> is the true friend.
> And the one who is not a prisoner to his senses
> is the true human. (140)

And if despite my explaining the situation at such length, the master does not listen out of attachment for Sanjeevaka, then I, the poor servant, am not to blame. For:

> A king lost to desires and attachments
> does not care for good counsel
> and does what he pleases
> like an elephant gone rogue.
> But when his pride goes before a fall,
> he forgets his own fault and
> heaps blame on his servants. (141)

Pingala then thought to himself:

> 'One should not punish a person
> on the instigation of another.
> Let me find out for myself
> and act accordingly. (142)

For it has been said:

> To honour or punish
> without first checking the virtues or vices of a person
> is self-destructive,
> like fingering a snake in the mouth.' (143)

Thinking in this way, he then spoke aloud: 'So what should I say to Sanjeevaka?' Damanaka rushed to reply: 'No, no, don't do that, oh master. That will spill the beans. And it has been said that:

> A secret, like a seed, should be protected at all costs
> and not exposed in the least
> for if exposed, it becomes impossible
> to achieve fruition. (144)

And further

> Some deeds worth doing
> must be done at the soonest
> or they are lost to time. (145)

So, by all means, let us accomplish the task with vigour. For

> Just as a cowardly warrior
> cannot last in battle for long,
> a secret strategy does not stay secret for long either,
> and then flops. (146)

Further, even after coming to know of his treachery, to admonish him and then be friends again would be even more of a blunder. Because:

> One who desires to be friends again with a person
> who has betrayed him once
> invites his death.' (147)

But the lion said: 'First find out what exactly Sanjeevaka can actually to do to us.' Damanaka responded:

> 'How can capacity be ascertained
> without knowing who is superior?
> See how a little lapwing bird

troubled the mighty sea.' (148)

The lion asked what that was about. So Damanaka began to narrate.

THE TENTH STORY

There lived a pair of lapwing birds on the shore of the Southern Sea. Once the female, who was with child, asked her husband to find a quiet place suitable to lay eggs. The husband said: 'Sweetheart, isn't this very place perfect?' She replied that it wasn't because the sea tide swept right up to where they lived. The husband chafed and asked: 'Am I any less mighty than the ocean that it dare trouble me?' His wife laughed and said: 'My dear, there's a world's difference between you and the ocean. But:

> It is not easy in this world to correctly estimate oneself.
> One who can, never comes to grief. (149)

> Further, to compete with one far stronger is suicidal
> just like attempting something inauspicious,
> opposing one's own friends,
> and trusting women.' (150)

However, reluctantly following her husband's advice, she laid her eggs at that very place. Having heard their conversation earlier, the ocean decided to test the male bird by washing away the eggs. Distraught, the female lamented to her husband: 'My dear, look! My eggs have been destroyed!' Her husband replied: 'Sweetheart, don't worry,' and then set off with all the other birds to their king, Garuda, the eagle. Once there, he narrated the events to Garuda saying, 'Oh master, innocent as I was, the ocean entered my own home and harassed me for no fault of mine.'

On hearing him, Garuda approached his Lord, God Narayana, the creator and preserver of the universe, and requested his intervention. The Lord duly commanded the ocean to return the little bird's eggs and the ocean humbly complied. 'And this is why I say capacity cannot be ascertained without knowing who is superior,' concluded Damanaka.

King Pingala however asked: 'How can we know that Sanjeevaka has turned disloyal?' Damanaka replied: 'When he comes charging at you, striking his mighty horns into the earth, then all will become clear to you.' So saying, Damanaka went off to Sanjeevaka and once there, approached him slowly, as if crestfallen. Sanjeevaka courteously enquired of him if all was well. Damanaka replied: 'When is anything well for a servant?

> Servants of the king are slaves.
> Their wealth is not their own.
> They are always heavy of heart
> and in perpetual danger to their lives. (151)

Further:

> Who is ever dear to the king?
> Just as who has lived forever?
> Who has not been tempted by a woman?
> Who has gained wealth but not airs?
> And who has escaped unscathed from the grip of villains?' (152)

Sanjeevaka said: 'Friend, please explain.' Damanaka replied: 'Wretched me, what will I explain? See:

> I have no idea what to do
> just like one drowning in the ocean
> can neither hold on nor let go

a serpent who lifts him out of the water. (153)

Torn between the trust of the king
and the impending death of a friend
what do I do, where do I go?
I am devastated.' (154)

So saying, he sighed deeply and sat down. Sanjeevaka said: 'Please tell me everything.' Damanaka then spoke in a low voice, 'Though one shouldn't reveal the king's secrets, you came here on trust, at my saying. So I must do the right thing and tell you the truth. Infuriated, the king has declared that he will kill you and feed you to his family.' Sanjeevaka was stunned and grieved to hear this. Damanaka again spoke: 'Please don't be sad. Act according to the situation.' Upset, Sanjeevaka thought to himself: 'He's right. And there's no way to know yet if this is his doing or not. Because:

Women prefer bad boys.
So too does the king heed the undeserving.
Like wealth collects with the miser
and rain falls most over sea and mountain. (155)

What's more, some villains preen and thrive
from the patronage of the king
just as black collyrium shines
in the eyes of beauteous women.' (156)

So thinking, Sanjeevaka spoke aloud: 'What jeopardy!

The king is not pleased
even if served with all sincerity.
This is indeed the only deity
that is annoyed when appeased. (157)

There is no figuring this one out. For look:

> If one is angry for a reason,
> they can be won over by removing that cause.
> But one who is angry for the heck of it,
> how can they ever be placated? (158)

What wrong did I ever do the king? Or perhaps unmerciful kings lash out for no reason at all.'

> Damanaka said: 'Indeed, that is the case. Listen:
> Some people turn enemies with their friends and well-wishers
> but continue to be friends with enemies.
> Unpredictable are some characters
> and serving them is harder than penance. (159)

> Many a good deed are lost on the wicked.
> Many a wise word are wasted on the fool.
> Many sound suggestions are no use for the stubborn.
> Many are the brains that are destroyed by the imbecile. (160)

> Happiness is never without its pitfalls.
> See how the sandalwood tree houses a serpent,
> the lotus pond an alligator,
> and the king's court the wicked. (161)

> Indeed, no part of the sandalwood tree
> is free from infestation by villains.
> Snakes at the root, bees on the flowers,
> monkeys on the branches, and bears on the treetop. (162)

It seems to me that our lord is sweet of tongue but deceitful at heart. Because:

> Only the wicked know how to enact such a drama
> where they wave at you from afar, look at you adoringly,
> share their seat with you, embrace you warmly,
> and listen to you attentively,
> all the while full of trickery and deceit within. (163)

Indeed, the Lord has provided a solution for every problem in this world:

> a boat to cross the ocean, a lamp to light up the darkness,
> a fan to beat the heat, and a goad to control the rogue elephant.
> But even the Lord is helpless, it seems, to rid the wicked
> of their nature.' (164)

Sanjeevaka sighed again and said: 'This is so wrong! How can a lion kill a grass eater like me?

> There can be a contest only between
> people of equal resources and strength.
> How can the weak and the mighty compete?' (165)

After a pause he again said:

'I don't know who has turned the master against me. But one should fear a king once he is displeased. Because:

> Who can mend the glasslike heart of a king
> once it is shattered by a minister
> through some deed of his? (166)

> The rage of a king is like a thunderbolt
> except that the latter strikes just one spot
> but the king's anger devastates all directions. (167)

So, it is better to die in battle than face this. Nor would it be proper for me to now submit to his orders. Because:

> A brave warrior in battle
> Obtains happiness either way,
> by killing his foe or by going to heaven.
> Rare are these two advantages to possess. (168)

And now is the time to fight.

> When by not fighting, death is certain,
> and the only hope of staying alive
> is through battle.
> Such a situation is time for battle, according to the learned. (169)

> An astute person prefers to do battle and die
> when he is unable to secure his interests
> without a fight. (170)

> If he wins, he rules. If he dies, he attains heaven.
> The body is transient and destructible in any case.
> So why hesitate from battle?' (171)

Deciding thus, Sanjeevaka said: 'Oh friend, tell me, how will I know he intends to kill me?' Damanaka replied: 'When you see Pingala swish his tail, bare his fangs, and raise his paw to strike, that's when you must show your prowess too. Because:

> If you do not exude vigour
> anyone can defeat you.
> Don't people walk all over ash and embers
> that have run cold! (172)

But please keep all this to yourself, otherwise we will both be destroyed.' So saying, Damanaka returned to Karataka, who asked what had happened. Damanaka replied: 'The two are now enemies.' Karataka said: 'No doubt! Because:

Who possibly is the friend of the wicked?
Who doesn't begging annoy?
Who doesn't turn arrogant from wealth?
And who isn't good at performing evil deeds? (173)

The cunning corrupt the rich for their own gain.
Their audacity knows no limits, like a raging fire.' (174)

Damanaka then went to Pingala and said: 'Lord, that crook is coming, be alert,' and then made him swish his tail, lift his paw, and bare his fangs. On seeing his changed demeanour, Sanjeevaka too assumed his aggressive pose. The two went to battle and ultimately the lion killed Sanjeevaka.

Immediately remorseful and exhausted, Pingala sat down wearily and lamented: 'Oh, what have I done!

Like the lion who kills an elephant, the king
who does wrong
incurs the sins of his actions
while others enjoy his kingdom. (175)

It is better to lose a piece of your kingdom
than to lose a talented and trusted follower,
for the kingdom can be won back
but the follower is gone forever.' (176)

Damanaka came up and asked: 'Master, what is this new approach where you repent the killing of a foe?

A king who desires sovereignty
must eliminate any danger to his life
be it his father, brother, son, or friend. (177)

A wise person learned in the four goals of life
must not be so given to pity.

For a compassionate person,
it would become difficult to consume even
a morsel of food. (178)

Forgiving a friend or a foe
behoves only the sage.
A king forgiving a wrongdoer
is a disaster! (179)

In any case, one who has committed the sin
of coveting the master's throne
through pride and greed
must pay with his life, no less! (180)

And, an excessively kind king
a greedy Brahmin,
an unbridled woman,
an indecent follower,
an insolent servant,
a careless officer,
and an ingrate,
these must all be forsaken forthwith! (181)

A king's policies must, especially, be variegated
like those of a whore:
sometimes honest, sometimes not,
sometimes harsh, sometimes soft,
sometimes violent, sometimes tolerant,
sometimes acquisitive, sometimes generous,
sometimes extravagant, sometimes restrained.' (182)

His grief thus assuaged, Pingala revived and ascended the throne. Damanaka cheered him on lustily and lived happily ever after.

♦

Vishnusharma then spoke: 'Thus you have heard the exposition on Losing Friends.' 'We have indeed, thanks to you, and are delighted,' cried the princes. The teacher then said:

> May the seeds of conflict take root
> in the homes of your enemies.
> May the wicked perish day by day.
> May your kingdom flourish.
> And may the young always shelter
> in the shade of these delightful
> words of wisdom. (183)

And here ends the second book of the *Hitopadesha*, titled Losing Friends.

BOOK THREE

Waging War

When the storytelling resumed, the princes said: 'Oh master, being royal princes, we are curious to hear about waging war.' Vishnusharma replied: 'Certainly, I will narrate what is of interest to you. Here goes:

> In the battle between swans and peacocks,
> the crows penetrated the den of the enemy
> and, winning their trust,
> deceived the swans.' (1)

'How was that?'
So Vishnusharma began to narrate.

THE FIRST STORY

There is a pool by the name of Padmakeli in the Karpura Island. There lived a swan by the name of Hiranyagarbha (Golden Womb). He had been anointed king by all the birds. Because:

> Subjects without a good king
> collapse like a boat without a boatman,
> adrift in the ocean. (2)

And, further,

> the king protects the people
> and the people pay taxes to strengthen the king.
> When the king is strong, so is the protection.
> Without that, life is insecure and uncertain indeed. (3)

Once, the royal swan was sitting gladly on his lotus throne, surrounded by his family. A stork named Dirghamukha (Long Beak) arrived from another country and sat down. The king said: 'Oh Dirghamukha, where have you come from and what news do you bring?'

The stork said: 'Oh king, there is something urgent and I have rushed to convey it to you. In Jambudvipa, there is a mountain called Vindhya. A peacock, Chitravarna (Pretty as a Picture), the king of birds, is resident there. His followers once spotted me pecking off the floor of the Dagdha Forest and asked who I was and from where I came. I told them that I am a follower of the victorious king of Karpura Island, Hiranyagarbha, the royal swan, and have come there exploring new regions. They then asked me which of the two kingdoms and kings was superior. I replied in a huff: "Where is the comparison? Karpura Island is like heaven and the royal swan is like a second Lord Indra. Why do you languish in this desert country? Come to our place." But they were furious to hear this. As it has been said:

> Feeding milk to snakes
> merely boosts their venom.
> Admonishing fools
> merely makes them angry, not happy. (4)

> One should advise only the intelligent, never the fool.
> Like when the birds advised the monkeys,
> they had to flee their own homes.' (5)

The king asked how that happened and so Dirghamukha began to narrate.

THE SECOND STORY

There was a giant silk cotton tree on the banks of the river Narmada. Birds built their nests in its branches and lived happily within them. One day, dark rain clouds filled the sky and it began to pour. A bunch of monkeys taking shelter under the tree started to shiver in the cold and wet. The birds were filled with pity and said to them: 'Hey, brothers:

> We have built nests from straws
> collected with our beaks.
> You have hands and feet both,
> yet you suffer so. Why?' (6)

The monkeys were annoyed to hear this. They thought: 'They live in airless nests and criticize us. Fine, let them do so till it rains.' Once the rain stopped, the monkeys climbed the tree and destroyed all the bird nests and smashed their eggs to the ground.

'And this is why I say advise only the intelligent, never the fool,' concluded Dirghamukha. The king asked: 'So what did the peacocks do then?' The stork resumed: 'The birds then asked in anger who had made you the king. I retorted with asking them who made their peacock the king. Hearing my words, they all rushed to attack me. I defended myself with valour. Because:

> Just as modesty does not suit women
> during the mating season
> so too valour, and not forgiveness,
> suits the warrior when faced with defeat.' (7)

The king laughed and said:

> 'They who don't first assess the difference
> in their strength and that of the enemy

are trifled with by enemies. (8)

Just like the donkey in tiger's skin
grazed long in the field of grain
but was given away
by the sound of his braying, and killed.' (9)

'How did that happen?' asked the stork. So, the king began to narrate.

THE THIRD STORY

There lived in the city of Hastinapura a washerman by the name of Vilas. His donkey was all skin and bones from the excessive loads he had to carry on his back. So, the washerman decided to drape a tiger skin on the donkey and leave him in the forest near a lush field of grain. Mistaking him for a real tiger from afar, the owners of the field kept their distance.

Then one day, one of the field keepers, wearing a beige coloured blanket, took up a bow and arrow and sat down in wait in the field. Seeing him, the donkey, now fattened up on all the grain and full of himself, mistook him for another one of his own kind and charged at him, braying out loud. The field keeper immediately understood what had happened and shot the donkey dead in a trice.

'This is why I say the donkey was given away by his braying and killed,' concluded the royal swan.

But Dirghamukha continued: 'The birds turned on me saying, "Oh you sinful stork, you peck in our fields yet you abuse our master? You don't deserve to be forgiven." They began to gnash their beaks at me and said: "You fool, your king, that swan, is naive, he doesn't deserve to rule. Because a naive man knows not how to protect wealth even if it is placed right in his hands. How can he then protect his kingdom? And you too are a frog in the well who doesn't know any better and so recommends such a master. Listen, you:

> Only a giant tree with immense shade and laden with fruit
> is worthy of being served.
> Even if by ill luck there is no fruit,
> the shade will never be forfeited. (10)

> One must never serve inferior people,
> only always the great.
> For in the hands of the liquor-seller's wife
> even pure milk is taken for liquor! (11)

> It is also stupid to praise the qualities
> of one who lacks any.
> It diminishes your own worth
> like an elephant captured in a mirror. (12)

> Under a powerful king,
> your interests can be protected
> by sheer association.
> Just as the rabbits lived happily ever after
> thanks to the moon." (13)

I found myself asking how that happened. So, the birds began to narrate.'

THE FOURTH STORY

Once in the monsoons when the rains failed, a thirst-ravaged herd of elephants said to their leader: 'Oh master, how do we survive now? Forget us, there's no water for even small animals to bathe. We are half dead. What do we do, where do we go?'

The king, however, led them to a clear pool nearby that he knew about.

As the herd of elephants went to and from the pool every day, little rabbits that lived in its vicinity were willy-nilly crushed under their feet. One of them, by the name of Shilimukha, grew worried: 'This thirsty herd will keep coming here and trampling our family out of existence.' 'Don't worry, I will find a solution,' said an old rabbit named Vijaya and, determined, he went off to the elephants. Along the way he wondered how exactly to approach the herd. Because:

> An elephant's mere touch
> a snake's mere breath
> a king even as he protects
> and a wicked man even as he laughs—
> kills! (14)

So let me climb a hill and then address the leader of the herd. As he did so, the king of elephants asked him who he was and from where he had come. The rabbit replied: 'I am a rabbit and I have been sent to you by the Moon God.'

'What for?'

Vijaya replied:

> 'Assured of protection to his life
> an ambassador always
> speaks the truth
> even if threatened by weapons. (15)

So, I now speak with the Lord's order. Listen, you have done a bad thing by expelling these rabbits who are protectors of this pool of the Moon God. They have been under the Moon's protection since time immemorial, which is why I am also famous by the name of Shashanka.'

No sooner had he said this than the king of elephants quickly blurted out in fear: 'This was unintentional. It won't happen again.' So Vijaya said: 'If that's the case, bow to the furious Moon God quavering in the pool and depart.' The elephant king did as he was told and the rabbit, accompanying him to the pool, pretended to address the image of the moon in the clear water and said:

'Oh Lord, this elephant has erred unintentionally, please forgive him. He will not repeat what he has done.' Saying so, he saw off the herd of elephants.

'And this is why we say that sometimes pretence gets the job done easily,' said the birds.

I, however, said: 'But our king, the royal swan, is highly capable and valorous. He deserves to rule the three worlds, not just the earth.' This aggravated the birds once again, and calling me names, they dragged me to their king, Chitravarna, the peacock.

They bowed before the king and then told him: 'Pay heed, oh king. This wicked stork, though living in our kingdom, criticizes you and sings paeans to another.' On being asked for details by the king, they told him that I was a follower of Hiranyagarbha, the swan, and had come from Karpura Island.

The vulture who served as minister then asked me: 'Who is the prime minister there?' I replied: 'A Brahminy duck named Sarvagya (Omniscient One), who is well versed in all the scriptures.' The vulture said: 'Right. He is native to the place.

> A king should appoint as minister
> only a native from a good family,
> one versed in the ways of the dynasty,
> righteous and free from corruption and vices
> like drinking and gambling,
> a clever thinker, a famed scholar,

and one who can generate wealth.' (16–17)

At this point, a parrot spoke up: 'Karpura Island and several other such small islands are all a part of Jambudvipa itself and your rule extends there too, oh king.'

'That's right,' said the king. 'Because:
Just like the very young, the lazy, the lunatic,
the greedy, and the ambitious,
kings too covet unattainable objects.
How much more so that which is within reach?' (18)

I retorted: 'If one becomes king just by saying it, then our king Hiranyagarbha rules over Jambudvipa as well.' The parrot piped in: 'How is this to be settled?' I replied: 'By war alone.' The king scoffed and said: 'Then go tell your king to prepare for it.' I told him he should send his own messenger. The king then thought aloud: 'Who will go as messenger? For:

Only one devoted, talented,
incorruptible, clever, calm, adept at speech,
a Brahmin, and a knower of the enemy's weaknesses
should be a messenger.' (19)

The vulture said: 'Many are the candidates. But choose a Brahmin. Because:

He pleases his master and never covets his wealth.
And is as constant of character
as the blue colour of Shiva's throat.' (20)

The king said: 'Then the parrot must go. Oh parrot, please go with this stork and convey our intention there.'

'As you wish, my Lord,' said the parrot, 'But this stork is wicked. I won't go with him. As it has been said:

It is the good who have to bear the brunt
of the deeds of the wicked.
Though Ravana abducted Sita,
it was the ocean that was bound by Lord Rama. (21)

Indeed, one must never keep the company of crooks.
The goose and the quail lost their lives
from being with the crow.' (22)

'How was that?' The parrot began to narrate.

THE FIFTH STORY

On the road to Ujjaini there was a big fig tree. A goose and a crow lived there. Once in the summer, a tired traveller passing that way stopped under the tree and went off to sleep, dropping his bow and arrow beside him. After a while, the shade of the tree shifted from his face and the rays of the sun beat down instead. Taking pity on the traveller, the goose atop the tree spread his wings to shield his face again.

Sleeping comfortably now, the man's mouth soon fell open. Then the wicked crow, who couldn't bear to see others in comfort, shat in his mouth and flew off! The traveller woke in shock and looked up, only to find the poor goose there. In a rage, he shot the goose dead. 'And this is why I say one should never keep the company of crooks. I will also now narrate the story of the quail,' said the parrot.

THE SIXTH STORY

Once upon a time, all the birds flew to the seaside in connection with the pilgrimage of Lord Garuda, the divine eagle. Among them was a crow and a quail. The crow kept pecking curd out of the vessel that a travelling cowherd carried on his head. In time, the man placed the vessel on the ground and looked up, only to see the crow and the quail. Shooed off, the crow was swift to depart, but the poor innocent quail, slower of movement, was caught and killed by the cowherd. 'And this is why I say never keep the company of the wicked,' concluded the parrot.

But I said to him: 'Why do you feel this way, brother? I regard you just as highly as I do His Majesty.'

> 'That may be so. But:
> The words of the wicked,
> no matter how sweet,
> make one wary,
> just as flowers blooming out of season. (23)

And your villainy is evident from your very words, for you have provoked a war between these two kings. See:

> Only a fool will ignore what is writ large
> and get taken in by sweet remonstrances.
> Just like the carpenter who
> lifted his wife and her paramour on his head.' (24)

'What was that about?' asked the king. So, the parrot began to narrate.

THE SEVENTH STORY

There lived in the town of Yauvanshri (Splendour of Youth) a carpenter named Mandamati (Slow of Mind). He suspected his wife of being unfaithful to him but never actually saw her with her paramour. So, one day, he announced that he was going to another village and left, only to quietly return and hide under the bed in his house.

Believing the husband to be away, the paramour came home as soon as darkness fell. While they were dallying atop the bed, the wife by chance felt the touch of her husband hiding below and understood what had happened. Her face fell. Her lover asked her what was wrong and why she wasn't involved in love play as before.

She replied: 'You don't understand. My childhood love, my husband, has gone away to another place. Without him here, the entire village seems desolate to me. I worry whether he's eaten or where he'll sleep. My heart is bursting with concern for him.'

'Is your carpenter really that loving?' asked the lover.

The faithless wife retorted: 'Oh, you wicked man! What do you think? Listen:

> Regardless of whether the husband
> glares with anger or utters harsh words,
> a righteous wife always
> keeps a smile on her face. (25)

> And whether in a city or a forest,
> whether a good soul or an evil one,
> fortune smiles on
> the wife who loves her husband. (26)

> A husband is the most beautiful ornament
> that can adorn a woman.
> Without him, even a beauty
> loses all her charm. (27)

You, on the other hand, are a sinner. Attraction to you is due to fickleness of the heart and may not last. But my husband has full rights over me; he can even sell me or donate me to the gods or Brahmins. What more can I say—I live because he lives. If he dies, I swear I will burn myself on his pyre. Because:

The wife who follows in her husband's footsteps
attains heaven for ever and ever. (28)

And just as a snake charmer
draws out a snake from his lair,
so too does a good wife
draw her husband to heaven. (29)

And she who climbs the pyre with her husband's body on
her lap ascends to heaven even if she is a sinner.' (30)

Hearing all this from where he was, the carpenter was overjoyed at having such a sweet and devoted wife. In his happiness, he got up to dance, lifting the bed on his head together with the wife and her paramour on it!

'And this is why I say only a fool will get taken in by sweet remonstrances,' concluded the parrot.

'Then the king bade me farewell on my mission to you. And the parrot too is headed this way,' said the stork to Hiranyagarbha, the royal swan. 'Please decide what should be done.'

The Brahminy duck minister then smiled and told the king: 'The stork sure has performed royal service in a distant land. But, oh king, this is the problem with fools!

The wise say sacrifice yourself if needed
but don't foment trouble.
Fools, on the other hand, stir up a conflict
without any reason whatsoever!' (31)

The king said: 'What is the point of crying over spilt milk? Now do what must be done.' The duck replied: 'I will tell you my plan of action when we are alone. For:

Subtle changes in expression, colour, voice,

eyes, and mouth
give away one's intentions.
So, it's best to discuss secrets in private.' (32)

All the other birds then moved away and only the king and minister were left. The duck then began to speak: 'Oh king, I am convinced that the stork was instigated to start this war by someone from among our own ranks. Because:

Servants gain when the master is embattled
just as doctors gain when people are sick
and the clever gain at the cost of fools.' (33)

The king replied: 'That may be so, we can verify the cause later. First work out what is to be done now.'

'Oh king, first send a spy to ascertain the enemy's strength and his intentions.

The spy is truly the eyes of a king
through which he comes to know
what's afoot in his own kingdom
and that of others.
Without a spy, the king is blind! (34)

And he should take a second person with him so that he can base himself in the enemy kingdom while the other man relays back to us all the news and his scheme. It has been said:

In the guise of ascetics
spies should be posted at temples and pilgrimage spots
to acquire intelligence on the enemy kingdom. (35)

The best undercover agent is one who can move on land and in water. So, send the same stork as a spy! And another stork should go with him. And his family members should be held hostage in our palace—but discreetly. No one else should be told about this. For:

> Once multiple people are kept in the know,
> it isn't long before a secret becomes public.
> So, a king must entrust matters to only one person:
> the minister. (36)
>
> Listen, oh king. Once a secret scheme is spilled,
> the damage is irreversible.
> Knowers of niti will tell you this.' (37)

The king considered for a moment and said: 'I have obtained the perfect spy, it seems!'

'You have obtained victory in battle too then,' said the minister, satisfied.

In the meanwhile, the doorkeeper entered and, bowing to the king, announced the arrival of the parrot from Jambudvipa. The king turned to the duck, who said: 'Have him wait in the residence prepared for him and bring him later for an interview.' When the doorkeeper withdrew, the king exclaimed: 'War has arrived!' But the duck said: 'Lord, war should never be the first resort. Because:

> A minister who advises his master
> to rush to war
> and forfeit his kingdom
> is condemnable. (38)
>
> And, when victory is uncertain for both parties,
> never initiate war. (39)
>
> First try diplomacy, donation, or sabotage—
> all three together or one by one—
> to quell the enemy.

> Never war first. (40)
>
> Besides, it's all very well to cry war
> without even knowing the strength of the enemy
> or without having ever actually gone to war! (41)
>
> And just as men can't lift a boulder
> without the use of a lever,
> so too does prudence lie in employing
> a small ruse for a big gain. (42)

However, when war indeed is knocking at one's door, one must prepare for it. Because:

> Just as farming gives fruit
> only after long months of laborious preparation,
> so too does strategy bear results
> only when developed over time. (43)
>
> The great may fear adversity
> from a distance
> but face up to it bravely
> when it is at hand. (44)
>
> Panic is the biggest obstacle to success.
> Staying cool, even water cuts its way through rock. (45)
>
> This Chitravarna in particular is most powerful.
>
> And it is no sign of bravery
> to fight the powerful.
> Doesn't wrestling with an elephant
> bring certain death? (46)
>
> One who jumps into battle
> without waiting for the right moment

is a fool and akin to
an insect fluttering to its death. (47)

But one who understands strategy,
endures attacks like a tortoise
shrinking into its shell.
And, when the right moment comes,
rears up like a serpent ready to strike! (48)

A strategist is equipped to destroy
all enemies, big and small.
Like a river in spate sweeps away alike
a speck of dust and a giant tree. (49)

So, assuage the enemy's messenger for now and keep him waiting till your fortress is up and ready. Because:

A sniper atop a fortress
can vanquish many an enemy soldier.
So even a hundred warriors
can take on one lakh enemy forces.
The fortress, therefore, is paramount. (50)

A king without a fort
is the easiest to rout,
helpless much like a drowning man
fallen off his boat. (51)

A fort should be built
near a mountain, river, desert,
or a dense forest.
And must possess lofty towers,
a deep moat, all manner of weaponry,
and abundant stores of water. (52)

A fort should be expansive, difficult to negotiate,
stocked with food, water, and fuel,
and with means of ingress and escape.' (53)

The king then asked who should be entrusted with building the fort. The Brahminy duck replied:

'Every person should be deployed
according to their respective expertise.
Otherwise even an intelligent man
will falter at an unfamiliar task. (54)

So have the crane called for.'

When the crane arrived, the king commanded him to erect a fort speedily. The crane, however, said: 'Sire, I have already identified this lake for building a fort. I just need food materials to be supplied to that island in the middle of the water. Because:

Of everything hoarded, grain is the best.
For jewels cannot be eaten to keep one alive. (55)

And of all food items, salt is the best,
for without it all else tastes like cow dung!' (56)

The king then told him to quickly go and make all the arrangements.

Soon the doorkeeper returned with the message that a crow named Meghavarna (Colour of the Clouds) had come, along with his family, from Sinhala Island and wanted an audience with His Majesty. The king exclaimed: 'Oh wow. Crows are all-knowing and careful creatures. It will be good to have them on one's side.'

But the Brahminy duck said: 'That's very well, oh king. But crows roam all over the place and this one is bound to be mixed up with our enemy. How is he worth keeping on our side then? It has been said:

> Those who hobnob with the enemy
> instead of their own people,
> such fools end up being killed by the enemy
> like the blue jackal.' (57)

'What was that about?' asked the king. So, the minister began to narrate.

THE EIGHTH STORY

Once a jackal scrounging about near the city limits fell into a pot of indigo dye. Unable to extricate himself, he lay there pretending to be dead. The next morning, when the owner of the pot arrived, he took out what he thought was the carcass and threw it far away. The jackal sprang to life and ran off into the forest.

Once there, he considered his blue appearance and thought: 'I have now acquired a superior colour. Why should I not become king?' He then gathered together all the jackals and said: 'The goddess of the forest has with her own hands smeared the juice of herbs on me and anointed me king of the forest. So, from now onwards, you will all obey my instructions.' All the jackals, awestruck by his lovely blue colour, offered elaborate salutations and vowed to do as ordered.

By and by, his sovereignty was accepted by all the animals of the forest in the same way. First his own tribesmen, the jackals, helped spread his domain. Later, he inducted the tiger, lion, and others as ministers and commanders, and then, embarrassed of the jackals, he ejected them from his circle with disdain.

Seeing the jackals now distraught, an old one among them vowed to seek revenge. He told the others: 'He has humiliated us, the knowers of strategy and wise counsel. Let us bring about his end. The tiger and others don't know he is a jackal and, taken in only by his colour, have accepted him as king. Let us spill the beans and disabuse them of their wrong perception! Tonight, let us all gather near him and howl in unison. Before he knows it, he too will join in and be exposed.' And that is exactly what happened. Because:

> It is very difficult
> to shed one's true nature.
> If you make a dog king,
> will he stop chewing on shoes? (58)

Thus recognized by the tiger, the jackal was killed by it. So, it has been said:

> Just as fire burns a dried-up old tree from within,
> so too does the enemy
> infiltrate, conspire, and use his power
> to destroy us. (59)

'And this is why I say those who hobnob with the enemy do not deserve to be on our side,' concluded the Brahminy duck.

'Well,' said the king, 'even if that is so, one should still meet someone who has come from such a great distance and arrange for his comfortable stay.' The duck said: 'Oh king, the spies have also been despatched and the fort is ready. So, we should give an audience to the parrot as well. And:

> Chanakya killed King Nanda through a spy.
> So, a king must meet a messenger
> from a safe distance only
> and surrounded by his clever ministers.' (60)

A meeting was then arranged with the crow and the parrot. The parrot, with his neck upraised, took his seat and began: 'Oh Hiranyagarbha, the king of kings, Lord Chitravarna has ordered that if your life or your kingdom is dear to you, you will come and prostrate before him. Otherwise, prepare to depart.'

Furious, the royal swan cried out: 'Is there no one who will strangle this fellow here?' The crow, Meghavarna, shot up and offered to put the parrot to death. But Sarvagya, the Brahminy duck, soothed tempers and said: 'First, please listen to me.

> An assembly must always have elders in it.
> Elders must always speak of dharma.
> Dharma must always contain the truth.
> And there can be no truth where there is deceit. (61)

Dharma says the following:

> A messenger must never be killed
> even if he be an inferior being.
> For he is the king's voice
> and even if threatened
> speaks only what he is told to. (62)

> And why should one be offended
> by what a messenger says anyway?
> Immune from death,
> he says anything he likes.' (63)

The king and the crow were pacified. The parrot too got up to leave and was courteously bid farewell by the king. He flew straight to the king of the Vindhyas and bowed. Chitravarna asked him what the news was and what kind of country Karpura Island was.

The parrot replied: 'Oh king, suffice it to say that now we must prepare for war. Karpura Island is like heaven and its king is like Lord Indra.' Chitravarna then called an assembly of his veterans and said: 'Decide how this war is to be waged. For wage war we must. As it has been said:

> A contented king like a discontented Brahmin,
> and a shy prostitute like a shameless family woman,
> are all destroyed.' (64)

Then an old vulture by the name of Dooradarshi (The Farsighted One) spoke: 'Lord, it is not wise to wage war without good reason. Because:

> One should only wage war
> when one is sure of the devotion
> of one's friends and ministers
> and of their staunch hostility
> towards the enemy. (65)

> And one should only wage war
> when one is assured of gaining
> kingdom, gold, or friendship.' (66)

The king replied: 'Oh minister, first please evaluate my army and their competence. And please have an astrologer called to fix an auspicious time to set out on the campaign.'

'Even with auspicious timing, it is not right to suddenly take off,' said the minister. 'Because:

> Fools who rush to battle
> without first ascertaining
> the enemy's strength
> die by the sword for sure.' (67)

The king got irritated and said: 'Do not dampen my spirits, minister. Instead, advise on how to go about conquering the enemy.' The vulture replied: 'I will so advise but it must be followed. For:

> What is the use of good counsel
> if it is not followed by the king?
> Just like good medicine
> must be taken for it to help the patient. (68)
>
> But since a king's orders must never be disobeyed,
> I am going to advise based on what I have learnt. (69)

So, listen:

> Oh king, in rugged and risk prone spots,
> such as where there are rivers, mountains, and jungles,
> the commander-in-chief should move
> in formation with his forces. (70)
>
> The chief together with the best warriors
> should move in the front,
> while the womenfolk, you, the king,
> the treasury, and the weaker forces
> should occupy the middle ranks. (71)
>
> On either side the horses, accompanied by the chariots,
> and then the elephants, and right at the outer rim
> the infantry should be positioned. (72)
>
> The commander-in-chief should rally the weaker soldiers
> while the king should move with the ministers
> and the great warriors. (73)
>
> The king should ride an elephant
> in rough terrain as well as wet and muddy ground
> and in hilly areas,
> while he should ride horses in the plains
> and use a boat to cross waterbodies.
> And in all these places he must

always be accompanied by the infantry. (74)

It is also wise to use elephants in the rains
and horses in the summers and winters. (75)

Oh king, you must be alert and defensive
when marching in the mountains and difficult terrain.
Though guarded by your soldiers
it is you who must constantly be on vigil. (76)

Harass and destroy your enemy by advancing hard
against him.
And in unfamiliar regions
always send ahead the local tribals
to show the way. (77)

The treasury should always accompany the king
wherever he goes
because there is no sovereignty without the treasury
and you have to reward your brave warriors
with wealth. For who doesn't fight for a generous master? (78)

Oh king, humans are not slaves to each other,
they are slaves to wealth!
And wealth alone determines hierarchy. (79)

There must be unity on your side.
Each must protect the other.
And the weak links should be placed
in the centre and shielded. (80)

Oh king, keep the infantry at the head
so that it engages the enemy
and loots and kills. (81)

In the plains you should battle with chariots and horses,
in riverine areas with boats and elephants,
in spots covered with vegetation you should resort to bows and arrows,
and on level ground, use swords. (82)

Destroy the enemy's reserves of fodder, grain, water, and fuel
and demolish their moats and ramparts. (83)

The elephant is the supreme asset in a king's army
for he is an octuple warrior: his eight limbs—
four legs, two tusks, one trunk, and one tail—
can each wipe out the enemy. (84)

And in the middle of the military formation
come the horses
which are instrumental in battles in the plains.
So, the king with many horses
likely wins there. (85)

Even the gods cannot defeat horse riders.
For they acquire a commanding view of the battlefield. (86)

The first principle of warfare
is to bolster and protect the army.
And it is the task of the infantry
to seal off all routes of ingress and egress. (87)

The best army is the one with
warriors who are fearless, undaunted,
able riders, and hard-working,
just like the best of Kshatriyas. (88)

Oh king, the way men fight
for the honour of their master,
they do not even for wealth. (89)

A small but fierce force
is superior to a vast but cowardly one.
For to see the meek run from battle
lowers the morale of even the brave. (90)

Troops get disaffected when
they are not given their due, are not protected,
are not given positions of authority,
are not paid on time, or denied their share of plunder. (91)

A king who seeks victory
must give his men rest
before the charge.
A tired force is easily overcome in battle. (92)

There is no strategy quite as good
as creating discord
among the kinfolk of the enemy.
So, take pains to instigate the relatives of the king. (93)

Befriend the heir apparent or the minister
and sow seeds of dissension secretly
in the house of the enemy.
And chase down the powerful supporters
of the enemy king
by either killing them in battle
or capturing their men. (94–95)

And settle in your own kingdom
with gifts and honour
men captured from the enemy kingdom.

More the subjects, more prosperous your kingdom.' (96)

The king then spoke: 'What is the point of so much chatter?
One's gain and the enemy's loss.
This is the policy.
The intelligent swear by this alone.' (97)

The minister laughed and said: 'This is indeed true. But:

Unbridled might is one thing.
One directed by policy is another.
And they cannot coexist
just as light and darkness cannot exist together.' (98)

Then the king arose and set off for battle at the hour appointed by the astrologer.

The spy sent ahead then came to Hiranyagarbha and said: 'Oh king, Chitravarna has arrived. He has parked his army at a height atop Malaya Mountain and is waiting there. It is imperative to guard the fortress well since their minister is the vulture and I am sure he has already planted someone there.'

The Brahminy duck immediately spoke up: 'Oh king, that's bound to be the crow!'

But the king said: 'I doubt it. He has been here for so many days now and was ready to attack the parrot messenger. He seems enthusiastic to go to battle, in fact.'

'Even so, it is important to doubt a newcomer,' said the minister.

'Newcomers often bring good tidings. Listen,' said the king:

'Even an enemy who helps is a friend.
And a friend who does no good is an enemy.
Just like disease is caused by one's own body
but the antidote comes from the wilderness. (99)

The king Shudraka had a servant called Viravara.
He sacrificed his own son
though having been in the king's service
but a short while.' (100)

'How was that?' asked the duck. So, the king began to narrate.

THE NINTH STORY

Once upon a time I was in love with Karpuramanjari, the daughter of the royal swan Karpurakeli, who resided in the pleasure pool of King Shudraka. One day, a prince from another land, by the name of Viravara, arrived at the palace and addressed the doorkeeper thus: 'I am a prince in search of employment. Introduce me to the king, will you?' Later, he said to the king: 'Sire, if you have need for my services, please hire me.'

'What salary would you expect?' asked the king.
'Five hundred gold coins daily.'
'And what are your assets?'
'Two arms and the third my scimitar.'

'Sorry, this won't do,' said the king, and the prince walked away. Then his ministers said to the king: 'Hire him for a few days to ascertain his nature and whether at such an expense he will be good for you or is of no use.' Viravara was then recalled and paid and thereafter kept under the king's watch.

It turned out that Viravara donated half the salary to the gods and Brahmins and another quarter to the needy. From the last bit left he ate and took care of his necessities. For the rest, he served day and night at the king's palace, sword in hand, and would go home only when explicitly asked to do so by the king.

Then one night, on the fourteenth day of the dark fortnight, the king heard the sound of someone sobbing. He called out: 'Who is guarding the door?' and, learning it was Viravara, ordered him to find out where the sobbing was coming from. After Viravara left, the king reconsidered his order to send the prince all alone into the thick darkness and decided he, armed with his sword, better go after him out of the city.

Viravara meanwhile found the source of the sobbing: a beautiful damsel laden with ornaments. He asked: 'Who are you and why are you weeping?'

'I am the goddess of royal fortune. I have resided here under the auspices of the valorous king Shudraka for a long time. Now I must go away.'

'Where there is a problem, there is also a solution. Tell me how it can be arranged for you to continue here,' said Viravara.

The goddess replied: 'If you sacrifice your talented and virtuous son Shaktidhara to the Goddess Sarvamangala, I will stay on here forever.' So saying, she vanished.

Viravara then went straight to his house and roused his wife and son from sleep. He told them everything that had happened. Shaktidhara then said with joy: 'I am blessed, Father, to serve the master's kingdom in this way! Why delay? Self-sacrifice for such a purpose is highly praiseworthy. Because:

> A wise person should readily give up
> their wealth and their life
> to help others.
> Death is inevitable. So why not
> for a good cause?' (101)

Then Shaktidhara's mother spoke: 'If you don't do this, how else will you pay off the debt of such a handsome salary that has been given to you?'

Having so resolved, the three went right away to the goddess Sarvamangala's spot. Worshipping her, Viravara said: 'Oh Goddess, may you be pleased! Victory to King Shudraka! Accept this offering,' and beheaded his son.

But then he was assailed by thoughts of how he would live without his child, and so cut off his own head. Shocked and mourning the loss of both her husband and son, his wife too killed herself.

King Shudraka, who had witnessed all this, thought to himself:

> 'What a wretch I am!
> There are so many like me in this world.
> But there never was and never will be
> another like him. (102)

So, there is no point for me to continue in this kingdom bereft of such a man as Viravara.' And he lifted his sword to end his own life. Just then the goddess Sarvamangala held his hand and said: 'Son, I am pleased with you. Don't kill yourself. Your kingdom will endure on and on even after your time.'

But Shudraka, after bowing to her respectfully, said: 'Oh Goddess, what do I care for this kingdom or my life? If I am at all worthy of your grace, let Viravara and his family come back to life. Otherwise, I will certainly behead myself.'

The goddess said: 'Son, I am pleased with your devotion and your love for your servant. Go, may you be victorious. And may this prince also come alive together with his family.' And so saying, she vanished. The king discreetly removed himself from the scene before Viravara and his family awoke and returned to their home.

The next morning, the king asked Viravara about the night before. He replied: 'Oh king, the sobbing woman vanished when she saw me. Nothing else transpired.' Hearing this, the king wondered: 'Oh, how should I felicitate this great soul? He has all the qualities of a good human being. For:

> The generous should speak sweetly,
> the brave should never praise themselves,
> philanthropists should never reward the unworthy,
> and the loquacious should never be unkind.' (103)

The next morning, the king convened an assembly of all the important people of his kingdom and narrated what had happened. Applauding Viravara handsomely, he made him king of Karnataka. 'And so, I ask, is a foreigner always suspect? There are good, bad, and average kinds among them too,' concluded Hiranyagarbha.

The Brahminy duck then replied:

> 'He who declares wrong to be right
> in deference to the king's wishes
> is a bad minister.
> For it is okay for the king to be displeased
> but it is not okay for him to be destroyed! (104)
>
> A king whose doctors, teachers, and ministers
> are all yes men,
> he is soon divested of his wealth, his health,
> and his dharma. (105)

Listen, oh master:

> One should not assume one will obtain
> what another did by their good fortune.
> The greedy barber who murdered the beggar
> was himself killed.' (106)

The king asked: 'What?' So, the minister began to narrate.

THE TENTH STORY

There lived in the city of Ayodhya a Kshatriya named Chudamani (Crest Jewel). Desirous of obtaining great fortunes, he took to painstakingly worshipping Lord Shiva. When he had in this way reduced his sins, there appeared in his dream, through the grace of Lord Shiva, Kubera, the lord of wealth, who spoke thus: 'If early morning today, you shave and hide in a corner of your house with a stick in hand, you will soon see a beggar enter. If you beat him mercilessly with that stick of yours, he will turn into a pot of gold. You can live comfortably off it the rest of your life.'

And that's just what happened! But the barber who had come to shave the warrior witnessed the proceedings as well and decided to employ the same strategy to make money. He shaved and hid, stick in hand, every day in his house, awaiting the beggar. Then one day, a poor beggar did chance by and was killed by the barber through no fault of his own. As a result, the barber was executed for the crime of murder by the king's men. 'And this is why I say one should not assume one will obtain what another did by their merit,' concluded the minister.

The king spoke:

'How can one infer from a tale of yore
whether a new arrival today
is a friend or foe? (107)

Okay, let it go. Focus on what is at hand. Chitravarna is upon Mount Malaya—what do we do?'

The minister said: 'Lord, our spy reports that Chitravarna disregarded the advice of his venerable minister, the vulture.

So, it may still be possible to conquer that fool of a king. For it has been said:

> An enemy who is greedy, devious, lazy,
> untruthful, impatient, cowardly, or foolish
> and one who disrespects the brave—
> can be readily destroyed. (108)

And, further, before he lays siege to our fortress, send the commander-in-chief, the crane, to kill his forces stealthily through mountain and jungle routes. It has been said:

> A king must attack the enemy forces just when they are
> tired from long marches, sleepy from night-long vigils,
> stalled by difficult routes or fire,
> hungry and thirsty, drunk and inebriated, gluttonous,
> or ailing and famine-hit, attacked by thieves,
> small in number, put off by rain and wind,
> mired in mud or deep waters, and desperate to escape.
> (109–12)

So let our forces take what chances they get to attack and loot that careless one's army.'

In this way a number of Chitravarna's soldiers and officers were killed. Panicked, Chitravarna then addressed his minister Dooradarshi thus: 'Oh sire, why do you neglect and humiliate me so? Have I ever been discourteous to you? Like it has been said:

> One must never be cruel
> just because one has acquired a throne.
> Cruelty repels fortune
> just as old age chases away beauty,
> and one who is smart obtains fortune
> like a modest eater obtains good health.

> A healthy person obtains happiness,
> a hard worker obtains the full extent of knowledge,
> and a humble, well-mannered person
> obtains wealth, prestige, and dharma.' (113–14)

The vulture replied: 'Lord, please pay heed:

> Even a foolish king attains great riches
> through the counsel of wise men.
> Like a tree thrives
> from mere proximity to water. (115)

> A king's vices, on the other hand, include
> drinking, womanizing, hunting, gambling,
> unjustly seizing the wealth of others,
> and passing harsh judgments and sentences. (116)

> In any case, bravado without discernment
> and indecision can never attract great wealth.
> For treasures reside only where there is
> wisdom and valour. (117)

You went entirely by the enthusiasm of your army, which relies on bravado alone, and ignored my advice, speaking harsh words to me. This is the fruit of your actions. It has been said:

> Which ill-advised king does not face consequences?
> Which rotten food does not cause disease and pain?
> Which man's head does not turn from riches?
> Which man does not suffer from the misdeeds of his wife?
> And who does death not kill? (118)

> And, just like grief puts an end to joy,
> winter to autumn, light to darkness,
> ingratitude to obligation, and success to sorrow,

> so does wise counsel put an end to crises
> and ill advice to good fortune. (119)

I knew back then that this king is a fool, for why else would he block the cool light of wise counsel with a hailstorm of harsh words?

> What good can books of knowledge
> do to a man without brains?
> Just like a mirror is no use
> to one without eyes. (120)

Thinking thus, I sat quietly all this while.'

The king folded his hands respectfully and said: 'Sire! I erred. Now please advise me on how to escape here with what forces I have left and return to the Vindhyas.'

The vulture thought to himself: 'I must advise him somehow. For:

> One should control one's anger
> at the gods and teachers,
> Brahmins and cows,
> kings and children,
> and at the elderly and the invalid.' (121)

So, the minister smiled and said out loud: 'Lord, don't be afraid. Have faith and listen:

> It is in pacifying an enemy at war
> that the brains of a minister are truly tested,
> like those of a physician in a dreaded disease.
> Otherwise, anyone can claim to be wise
> when all is smooth sailing. (122)

> And, the little men panic at the littlest of tasks

while the great take on onerous tasks
but never panic. (123)

So, I will destroy the enemy fort and take you home to the Vindhyas with prestige intact.'

'How is this possible with what little is left of our forces?'

'Lord, everything is possible. Speed is of the essence for a conqueror. So quickly have their fort surrounded,' said the vulture.

Now, the stork who was sent as spy returned to Hiranyagarbha and narrated all. The king asked: 'Oh Sarvagya, what should be done now?' The Brahminy duck replied: 'First separate the strong from the weak in your ranks. Then reward them handsomely with gold etc. as per their competence. Because:

> The king who saves every rupee when he can
> and lavishes crores of rupees when he must
> is always victorious and prosperous. (124)

Further,

> Money is never wasted when invested in
> ritual sacrifices, weddings, calamities,
> and in destroying the enemy, felicitating a friend,
> gifting to loved women, donating to indigent relatives,
> and in acts that further your reputation. (125)

> Only a fool sabotages everything he has
> for fear of spending a little money.
> Does a merchant destroy his entire shop
> for fear of paying cess on it?' (126)

But the king queried: 'Why should excess expenses be incurred at such a time? It has been said to save up for a rainy day.'

'But what rainy day will befall the fortunes of your highness?'

'What if royal fortune departs?' asked the king.

'Hoarded wealth is also destroyed, oh king. Therefore, give up being miserly and reward your brave warriors with an open heart and honour,' said the minister. 'It has been said:

> Soldiers who are well honoured and taken care of,
> happy of heart and helpful to one another,
> and willing to die for their lord,
> they definitely trounce the enemy in battle. (127)

> Just five hundred of them with discipline and a sense of fraternity
> and committed to kill or be killed in battle
> are more than enough to get the better of
> even an army of great warriors. (128)

> Whereas everyone, even the virtuous,
> desert a fool, a crook,
> an ingrate, and a selfish person. (129)

> Indeed truth, valour, mercy, and generosity,
> these are the main qualities of a king.
> One devoid of these comes in for criticism from all. (130)

And at such a time you should first honour the ministers. It has been said:

> They who are committed to us
> and who rise with us and fall with us
> they alone should be appointed in charge
> of one's wealth and one's life. (131)

Because:

> The king with a rogue, a woman, or a child as minister
> will be swept by the winds of poor statecraft

and land up drowning in the ocean of work he must
attend to himself. (132)

Listen, oh Lord,

> They who are stable of nature, have faith in learning,
> and are affectionate towards their servitors,
> their rule will always prosper. (133)

> Those who rise and fall steadfastly with the king
> they are called ministers.
> The king must never dishonour them. (134)

> Pure-hearted, they alone lend a hand to steady
> a king wavering, intoxicated with pride.' (135)

At that moment Meghavarna, the crow, entered, and bowing before the king, spoke: 'Lord, the enemy is at our gates. Permit me to go out there and show my prowess and pay off my debt to you thus.'

'No, don't,' said the Brahminy duck, 'If we go out to fight, what is the point of the protective fortress?

> Just as a crocodile out of water is powerless,
> so too the valorous lion runs fearful on leaving
> the forest. (136)

Lord, please go and see to the battle yourself. Because:

> The king should lead from the front in war.
> Even a dog roars like a lion when his master goads
> him on.' (137)

So, they all went to the fortress gate and fought hard.

The next day, Chitravarna approached the vulture again and spoke: 'Sire, please fulfil your promise now.'

'Oh king, please listen to me first:
A fort with weak walls, a small and timid force,
a foolish and inebriated commander, and weak defences
is doomed. (138)

But that is not the case here.

So, these are the four ways out:
send in a saboteur to sow seeds of discord,
lay siege for months,
attack relentlessly,
and show utmost bravery. (139)

Here we must choose according to our capacity.' So saying, the vulture whispered stratagems into the king's ear.

Then one day, while fierce battle raged outside the fort, crows within quietly set fire to it. Seeing huge flames issue in all directions, and hearing their cries of 'the fort has been taken!', the brave warriors of the royal swan and all residents of the fort escaped into the surrounding lake. Because:

When required, a good strategy, great bravery,
heroic fighting, as well as fleeing for one's life
must be resorted to without a moment's hesitation! (140)

The royal swan, however, being slow of movement, was, along with his aide the crane, encircled by Chitravarna's general, the cock. The king addressed the crane: 'Oh general, why do you put your life in danger because of me? You can still leave. Go, jump into the water, and save yourself. And, with Minister Sarvagya's permission, anoint my son Chudamani my successor.'

'Don't say such awful things, my Lord!' said the crane, 'Till the sun and moon are in the sky, may Your Highness be ever victorious. I am but a servant of the fort; if the enemy has to enter it, let it be over my dead body.

> A kind, giving, and virtuous master is obtained through great penance.' (141)

The king said: 'That is true. But:

> It is just as difficult to obtain a noble, true, intelligent, and loyal servitor!' (142)

The crane said: 'Listen, Lord:

> When there is hope of survival after leaving battle,
> it may be all right to leave.
> But when death is certain, why demean oneself
> and tarnish one's reputation? (143)

> Further, in this ephemeral world
> dying for the sake of another
> is a rare blessing. (144)

> King, minister, territory, fort, treasury,
> army, allies, and subjects—
> these are the elements of sovereignty. (145)

You are the king! You must be protected at all times! Because:

> Subjects can never survive without their king
> no matter how prosperous they may be.
> Just as when life exits the body
> there is nothing left for Dhanvantri, the great physician,
> to do. (146)

> Like the lotus blooms when the sun rises
> and droops when it sets,
> the living world knows death when the king dies
> and life when he lives.' (147)

By then the cock inflicted severe wounds on the royal swan. Instantly, the crane threw himself over the king's body and pushed him to safety into the water. The cock then took to attacking the crane and though he fought valiantly, he was soon killed. Chitravarna then triumphantly entered the fort, looted its treasures, and left for his abode.

◆

After a moment, the princes spoke: 'That crane was the one pious person in the king's force who sacrificed his own life to save the master. It has been said:

> All cows give birth to calves of the same dimensions.
> Rare is the cow who births a grand bull.' (148)

Vishnusharma said: 'May that great soul, the crane, attain heaven. Like it is said:

> Brave warriors who give up their lives in battle
> for the honour of their kings,
> those loyal and grateful men
> always go to heaven. (149)

Thus, you all have heard about Waging War.'

'And we greatly enjoyed it too!' said the princes.

Vishnusharma then said: 'May that always be the case.

> And may kings like you
> never have to battle armies.
> May your enemies instead,
> blown away by the sheer force of strategy,
> hide away in mountain caves.' (150)

And here ends the third book of the *Hitopadesha*.

BOOK FOUR

Making Peace

When the storytelling resumed, the princes requested that having heard about the waging of war, they now wanted to hear about how peace was won. Vishnusharma said: 'Of course, please listen. And the first lines of the book on winning peace are:

> After fierce battle had been fought
> and both armies lay dead or dying,
> the vulture and the Brahminy duck
> got together and achieved truce in no time. (1)

The princes asked: 'Oh! How was that?' So Vishnusharma began to narrate.

THE FIRST STORY

The royal swan asked: 'Who put fire to our fortress? Was it the enemy or one of our own put up to it by the enemy?' The Brahminy duck replied: 'Oh king, that strange friend of yours, Meghavarna, the crow, together with his family, is nowhere to be seen now! So, it does seem to be his doing.' The king paused a moment and said: 'This is the result of my own karma. Like it has been said:

> Fate is at fault here, not any minister,
> for at times
> even the best laid plans
> are foiled by ill luck.' (2)

The minister said: 'But it has also been said:

> Fools run into trouble
> and blame their luck.
> They don't recognize it to be
> the fruits of their own actions. (3)

And further:

> He who ignores the wise counsel of good friends,
> such a fool dies,
> just like the tortoise who fell off the wood.' (4)

The king asked how that happened. So, the minister began to narrate.

THE SECOND STORY

There once was a pond by the name of Phullotpal (Blooming Lotuses) in the country of Magadha. Two swans by the name of Sankata (Trouble) and Vikata (Difficulty) had been living there for a long time along with their friend, a tortoise named Kambugriva (Neck like a Shell). Once, some fishermen arrived and decided that the next morning they would catch fish and tortoise in the lake. Having heard their words, the tortoise approached his friends, told them the situation, and asked for their counsel. The swans said: 'Let's think about it and then see what to do tomorrow.' The tortoise, however, disagreed. He said: 'No, that would be risky, I sense real danger here. For it has been said:

> They who anticipate the future and think ahead
> and they who rise to the occasion when it arises
> are happy.

But those who say, "We'll see, whatever will be will be"—
die!' (5)

The two friends asked what he meant. So, the tortoise began to narrate.

THE THIRD STORY

Once, long back, when fishermen visited the same lake, three resident fish put their heads together to think. The one named Anaghatavidhata (Anticipate the Future) decided to move to a different lake and left. The one called Pratyutpannamati (Rise to the Occasion) said: 'There is no certainty right now about what will happen. So, I will act according to what happens. For it has been said:

> He who solves a problem as it arises
> shows true intelligence.
> Like the merchant's wife who hid her lover
> right under his nose.' (6)

Hearing this, the third fish, by the name Yadbhavishya, (What Will Be Will Be), asked how that happened. So, Pratyutpannamati began to narrate.

THE FOURTH STORY

Once upon a time, there lived a merchant named Samudradatta in the city of Vikramapura. His wife, Ratnaprabha, was in an illicit relationship with her servant. One day, Samudradatta caught her kissing the servant. Ratnaprabha, however, quickly went up to her husband and said: 'Beloved, this servant has been stealing camphor from the house all these days. I just smelt his mouth and discovered it.'

The servant protested and said: 'Oh master, where the mistress of the house constantly checks and smells the mouths of servants, how can any servant ever stay?' and so saying he got up to leave. Believing the yarn, the merchant pressed the servant not to go and persuaded him to stay on. 'And this is why I say he who solves a problem as it arises shows true intelligence,' concluded Pratyutpannamati. But then Yadbhavishya spoke:

> 'What will be, will be.
> And what is not to be, will never be.
> Why don't you drink of this wisdom
> that quenches all worry?' (7)

The next morning when the fishermen came, Pratyutpannamati, snared in their net, pretended at first to be dead. Then when he was released from the net by the fishermen, he dashed and dove into the water. Yadbhavishya, however, was caught and killed by the fisherfolk.

'And this is why I say that they who anticipate the future and think ahead, and they who rise to the occasion, are happy. But those who say whatever will be will be—they die!' concluded the tortoise. 'So please find a way to get me to another lake.'

The two swans considered the matter and replied: 'Yes, it is better for you to move. But is it safe for you to travel over land?'

'Please take me by the aerial route with you,' pleaded the tortoise.

'But how?'

'The two of you hold a piece of wood between your beaks and I will grab it in the middle with my teeth. You can then safely fly me to my destination.'

The swans said: 'Yes, this is possible. But:

A wise person should not just think of strategies
but also of possible loopholes.
See how the mongoose ate up all the fledglings
even as the foolish crane looked on.' (8)

The tortoise asked how that happened, and so the two swans began to narrate.

THE FIFTH STORY

Towards the northern direction, atop a hill named Gridhrakuta, there grew a large peepal tree. A number of cranes lived on it. The serpent who lived in the burrow under the tree would routinely devour the young ones of the cranes. On one such occasion, when the cranes were weeping and mourning the death of their babies, one of them said: 'Let's do one thing. Spread out dead fish in a line from the burrow of the mongooses till the burrow of the serpent. Greedily consuming the fish, the mongooses will wind their way to the serpent and, true to their nature, kill it.' And that's exactly what transpired.

Later, however, the mongooses were drawn to the sound of the gentle chirpings of the newborn cranes atop the tree. So, they climbed the tree and ate up the baby cranes as well. 'And this is why we say a wise person should not just think of strategies but also of possible loopholes,' concluded the storks. 'Seeing us fly you off, people below are bound to exclaim, and you may open your mouth to reply, and will certainly fall to your death then. So, it may be best if you stay put here.'

But the tortoise was adamant. He said: 'Am I a fool? I won't reply. I won't utter a word.'

As the two storks took off with the tortoise, a bunch of

cowherds ran after them, mocking. Some said, 'If this tortoise falls off, let's roast and eat him right here' while others suggested they take him home to dine on. Hearing all this, the tortoise forgot all about the wise precaution and yelled 'Get lost!' No sooner than he did that, he fell to the ground and was killed in a trice.

'And this is why I say the fool who ignores the wise counsel of good friends dies,' concluded the Brahminy duck.

The messenger stork happened to arrive just then and said: 'Oh king, I had already warned you to have the fortress inspected from time to time. You didn't and that's why you are paying the price. Meghavarna, tutored by Chitravarna's vulture, set fire to the fortress.'

The king sighed deeply and said:

'The person who trusts an enemy
out of affection or a sense of obligation
is like the man who falls asleep atop a tree
and awakens only when he falls right off.' (9)

The messenger continued: 'On setting fire to your fort, when Meghavarna returned to the enemy side, Chitravarna was mighty pleased and said: "Have this Meghavarna anointed the king of this Karpura Isle!" As it has been said:

The servant who gets the job done
must never go unrewarded.
He should be feted with gifts, smiles, and sweet words.'
(10)

The duck then asked: 'What happened after that?'

'After that, Prime Minister Vulture spoke: "Oh Lord, this is not appropriate. Reward him in some other way if you must. For:

> Obliging a mean-spirited person
> is short-lived and soon forgotten.
> Just like markings in the sand
> or advice to the thoughtless
> are gone in no time. (11)

You should never appoint a pygmy to a high position. For it has been said:

> An inferior person given a high post
> soon turns to treachery
> and wants to kill his master.
> Like the mouse who tried to kill the sage
> on attaining the powers of a tiger.'" (12)

When prodded by Chitravarna to explain how, the minister began to narrate.

THE SIXTH STORY

In Sage Gautama's sacred forest, there lived a saint by the name of Mahatapa (Great Penance). One day he caught sight of a baby mouse dropped from a crow's beak. Compassionate by nature, the saint brought up the mouse, feeding him grain. Attacked by a cat once, the mouse fled to safety in the saint's lap. The rishi granted him a boon, transforming him into a cat himself! But then he was chased by a dog. And so, the rishi made him into a dog, who however took fright at a tiger. The sage then transformed the mouse into a tiger.

The sage continued to regard the tiger as that little mouse he knew. People around stared at the duo and exclaimed at how the sage had made the mouse into a tiger. Offended at this, the tiger thought to himself: 'So long as this sage lives, my ignominious origins will never be forgotten.' So thinking, he set off to kill him. Apprehending what had happened, the rishi turned the tiger back into a mouse! 'And this is why I say that an inferior person given a high post soon turns to kill his master,' concluded the minister. 'Nor is this easy to do.

> See how the greedy crane
> devoured all kinds of fish
> and was then easily killed by a crab.' (13)

On being pressed, the minister began to narrate.

THE SEVENTH STORY

There is a pond called Padmagarbha (Womb of Lotuses) in Malava. There, an aged crane once sat as if deep in contemplation. A crab said to him: 'What's this? Why do you sit here all hungry and thirsty?' The crane replied: 'Fish are the basis of life for me. But I have heard in the town that fishermen will soon come and kill them all. That will spell death for me, so I might as well practise starvation right away.'

The fish overheard this and decided to go seek his counsel on what to do to save their lives since he sounded their well-wisher at that moment. Since it is said:

> Ally with a well-wishing enemy
> rather than a malicious friend.
> For goodwill and malice alone
> are defining of friendship and enmity, respectively. (14)

The fish said: 'Oh crane, what is the way to save our lives?'

He replied: 'The only way is to move to another lake. I can shift you there one by one if you like.'

The fish agreed and the crane began to take away one fish at a time and consume it! Then the crab asked to also be shifted in this manner. Greedy for delicious crab meat, the crane took the crab and placed him there on the ground. The crab noticed the skeletons of the many fish that had been eaten and panicked: 'Oh God, I am such a fool, I am dead now! But no matter what happens, I am going to act exactly as the situation demands.' So saying, the crab bit the neck of the crane, killing it instantly.

'And this is why I say see how the greedy crane devoured all kinds of fish but was easily killed by a crab,' concluded the minister.

'But minister, here is what I had planned: When made king of Karpura Island, Meghavarna will bring to us all the choicest items from there as prestation. And we will delight in those sitting here in the Vindhyas. '

At this Dooradarshi, the vulture, laughed and said: 'Oh master,

> He who rejoices over
> what has yet to come to pass
> earns contempt
> like the Brahmin who smashed the vessels of clay.' (15)

'How was that?' the king asked, and so, the minister began to narrate.

THE EIGHTH STORY

There once lived in a town called Devikot a Brahmin named Devasharma. On the day of the spring equinox, he received as a gift from someone a jar of barley. Drowsy with the midday heat, he decided to rest in a potter's shed with his gift by his side and, stick in hand to ward off mice, began to daydream.

He thought: 'If I sell this jar of barley right now for

ten cowries, I can then buy with that money a number of earthenware, which if I sell off, I can in turn buy from the compounded profit, betel nuts, cloth, and other articles of luxury. And reselling those again and again, I will soon earn in lakhs and will then be able to marry four wives. Of the four, I will favour her who is the most beautiful and youthful. And if the other wives fight with her in envy, I will take a stick like this and beat them!' So thinking he swung his stick around, smashing the barley jar as well as a number of other pots there! Hearing the din, the potter rushed into the barn and abused the Brahmin, driving him out. 'And this is why I say he who rejoices over what has yet to come to pass, earns contempt,' concluded the minister.

Then the king spoke in private with the minister and said: 'Sire, please say what should be done.'

The vulture began:

'Ministers of arrogant kings
who head on the wrong path
earn ill repute
like the drivers of rogue elephants. (16)

Listen, oh king. Did we smash the fortress through our strength? No. Only through stratagem. If you ask me, let us return to our kingdom. Once the rains come, fighting on enemy soil will prove difficult for us as will returning home. So, sue for peace in the interest of your happiness and prestige. It will then be said that we conquered the fort but also hearts. This is my advice. Because:

One who puts dharma first
and not the likes and dislikes of the master
and speaks what is right even if it is unpalatable

he alone is the king's true adviser. (17)

Further, which sensible man will
trust his friend's forces, kingdom, honour,
and even himself
to the vagaries of battle? (18)

Victory in war is always uncertain
when fighting an equal.
So, it is best to make peace with such a rival.
Didn't the equally matched Sunda and Upasunda
do each other in?' (19)

'What?'

And so, the minister began to narrate.

THE NINTH STORY

There lived two magnanimous demons, Sunda and Upasunda. Once, they decided to conquer the three worlds and, towards this end, began to worship Lord Shiva, performing severe penance for a long, long time. Pleased, the Lord finally appeared before them and granted a boon. By a wondrous twist of fate, the two blurted out something quite different from what they had intended to ask for. They asked instead that Shiva grant them his wife Goddess Parvati!

Shiva was enraged, but bound by the necessity of keeping his promise, he granted Parvati to those foolish demons. Now those two, dazzled by her beauty, and quite blinded by lust and aggravation, began to fight with each other over her. Ultimately, they decided they should consult someone in authority. Learning of this, Lord Shiva himself took the form of an elderly Brahmin and showed up at their place.

The demons then asked the Brahmin: 'We have both gained this lady through our prowess. Which one of us does she belong to then?'

The Brahmin said:

'The Brahmin is venerated for his superior knowledge.
The Kshatriya for his strength and power.
The Vaishya for his wealth and riches.
And the Shudra is venerated for his service of society. (20)

Therefore, the two of you, following the nature of Kshatriyas, need to battle it out to decide.' The demons were happy at this prospect and immediately got down to wrestling each other. Being of equal prowess, however, they both ended up losing their lives. 'And this is why I say victory in war is always uncertain when fighting an equal. So, it is best to make peace with such a rival,' concluded the minister.

Chitravarna was miffed. 'Why didn't you say this right at the beginning?'

'My Lord, did you hear me out then? No! Even so, it is thanks to my prudence that this war has not begun in earnest yet. Hiranyagarbha is a good man. He does not deserve to be opposed and fought. It has been said:

One must transact peace with
seven types of people:
the honest, the good, the righteous,
the brave and the ever-victorious, battle-hardy ones,
and also the wicked and those with a number of allies. (21)

The honest will undertake the treaty truthfully
and never betray it.
And the good will remain honourable

even at the cost of their lives. (22)

If a virtuous king is attacked,
everyone will rise in his defence.
Strengthened by the love of his subjects
and his own just ways,
a righteous king is not easy to defeat. (23)

If one's destruction is imminent,
once should make peace even with the wicked.
For the good cannot survive without
dealing with the wicked. (24)

And just as a clump of bamboos
sticking together
is difficult to cut down.
So too a man with many allies
is difficult to vanquish. (25)

One must not challenge a powerful enemy.
For clouds never move in a direction
opposite to the wind. (26)

And an ever-victorious warrior,
like Parashurama who defeated all the kings,
is subserved by everyone always and everywhere.
So, allying with such a warrior
wins the friendship of
all the kings defeated by him too. (27–28)

So, Hiranyagarbha is fit in every way to make peace with,' said the vulture.

Hearing this whole narration from their spy, the Brahminy duck sent him off to gather more intelligence. Meanwhile, Hiranyagarbha asked the minister to elaborate on who all are unworthy of transacting peace with. The minister replied:

> 'Oh master, the following twenty kinds of people
> need never be compromised with:
> The young, the old and the ailing, the outcaste,
> the coward, the panic-struck, the greedy,
> or the one with a greedy minister. (29)
>
> The debauched, the one lost to gratification,
> the one who confides in many, the one who insults gods and Brahmins,
> and the one whose subjects are disaffected. (30)
>
> The unlucky, the fatalist, the drought-hit
> and the one bogged down by mutiny. (31)
>
> The one with many enemies,
> or residing in another's kingdom,
> the impulsive and heedless,
> and the unvirtuous one. (32)
>
> Never sign a treaty with any of these twenty kinds.
> For they are easy to defeat in actual battle. (33)
>
> A child is powerless and knows not the fruits of war,
> so his army does not stand up to fight for him.
> The old and the ailing lack in vigour and spirit
> and so automatically lose to the enemy.
> The outcaste is easy to defeat
> since his own caste men have taken away all his resources.
> The coward soon flees the battlefield
> and is deserted by his forces too. (34–37)
>
> The greedy and miserly king's men revolt
> while his own greedy followers

soon kill their master.
The king with disaffected subjects
is readily deserted by them.
The one lost to sense pleasures is the simplest to beat.
The one who confides in many
and lacks a decisive bent
loses the trust of his counsellors and ministers. (38–40)

The one who abuses gods and Brahmins
and the one who lacks good karma
are destroyed in the normal course.
The fatalist over-relies on luck
and neglects to act.
The drought-hit king and the one ravaged by mutiny
are powerless and lose with ease. (41–43)

The one residing in another's kingdom
is vulnerable
like the elephant in water
is easy prey for the crocodile who resides there.
The panic-struck and the one with many enemies
is perennially in trouble
wherever he goes. (44–45)

The king who goes to untimely battle on a whim
is destroyed, like the night-blind crow
is killed by the denizen of the night, the owl.
And the one lacking all truth and virtue
should never be trusted with a treaty
for he is bound to turn coat later. (46–47)

Moreover, let me spell out for you the other things a great man will ponder before he determines to go to war and win. These are the six policies: waging war, making peace, marching, halting, taking shelter, and duplicity. The five aims: making the right start, accumulating men and materials, choosing the right place and time, guarding against accidents, and securing the goal. The four strategies: appeasement, bribe, dissension, and coercion. And the three powers: willpower, the power of good counsel, and the power of divine blessings.

> The goddess of royal fortune
> who may elude even one who lays down his life
> goes running to the one who wields
> the knowledge of prudent conduct. (48)

It has also been said:

> The king who gives fairly of his wealth,
> and whose spies are secret and confidences well-guarded,
> and one who speaks sweetly to his subjects,
> such a king conquers the whole world
> till the ends of the earth.' (49)

The duck then continued: 'But since despite his minister's counsel to sue for peace with us, Chitravarna, haughty with victory, is still adamant, oh king, have our friend Mahabala—the stork and king of Sinhala Island—threaten Jambudvipa. Because:

> When a belligerent king with an effective force
> harasses the enemy, he too will be afflicted
> and more amenable, in his affliction,
> to making peace with us.' (50)

The king Hiranyagarbha immediately agreed and gave orders for Vichitra, a stork, to carry a secret missive from him to Sinhala Island.

Meanwhile, their spy returned once more and reported: 'Oh master, this is what else has transpired at Chitravarna's camp. The vulture told the king that he should check with Meghavarna, the crow, who spent a great deal of time at Hiranyagarbha's court and would know whether or not the latter is deserving of a peace treaty. The king called for Meghavarna and asked him about Hiranyagarbha and the Brahminy duck, his minister.

The crow replied: 'Oh master, the king Hiranyagarbha is like Yudhishthira himself, justice and goodness personified. And I have yet to see a minister like that Brahminy duck.'

'If that's the case, how did you manage to deceive them?'

Meghavarna laughed and said: 'Oh king

> Is it hard to deceive those who are trusting?
> What is the big deal in killing one
> who lies resting in one's lap? (51)

Listen, oh Lord, that minister had sized me up at once. But that king is very decent and was taken in by my fraud. As it has been said:

> Good people think everyone else is good too.
> And so, they are easily cheated by the wicked.
> Just like how the Brahmin was cheated by the crooks
> over a goat.' (52)

'What was that about?' the king asked. So, Meghavarna began to narrate.

THE TENTH STORY

Once in the forest of Gautama, a Brahmin undertook a fire sacrifice. For this he bought a goat from another village and carried it back on his shoulders. Seeing them, a group of three thugs decided to cheat the Brahmin out of the goat. They each hid behind a tree a mile apart from one another and awaited the arrival of the Brahmin.

As he approached, the first thug went up to him and said: 'Oh Brahmin, why are you carrying this dog on your shoulders?' The astonished Brahmin replied that it wasn't a dog but a goat and went on his way. In time, the second thug came up and said the same thing to him. This time the Brahmin put the goat down and stared at it intently for some time before uncertainly lifting it up again and setting off with some trepidation. Because:

> Good people often get taken in
> and second-guess themselves
> by the words of the wicked.
> Like this Brahmin who died
> much like Chitrakarna, the camel. (53)

The king asked: 'How did that happen?' So, he began to narrate.

THE ELEVENTH STORY

There once lived in a forest a lion named Marodkata. Among his followers were a crow, a tiger, and a jackal. One day, they came across a solitary camel and asked him how he had got separated from his herd. The camel told them his story upon which they took him and handed him over to the lion who set his fears at rest and even named him Chitrakarna.

Soon, however, when the aging lion could no longer hunt as well, his followers were driven by starvation to consider having the camel killed by the lion for them to eat. The tiger, however, said: 'Our master has assured him safety of his life. How can he kill him now?' The crow said: 'Our master is himself desperate for food right now, he will commit the sin. Because:

> A starving woman forsakes even her son.
> A starving serpent devours its own eggs.
> One hungry will commit any sin.
> The weak person knows no compassion. (54)

And further:

> The hungry, the exhausted, the incapable,
> the headstrong, the intoxicated, the angry,
> the greedy, the cowardly, the lustful,
> and the thoughtless person
> have no use for dharma.' (55)

Having so determined, they all trooped over to the king. Seeing them, the lion asked if they had found any provision for food. On being told that they had failed miserably, he said: 'How will we live now?' The crow replied: 'Sire, all this has happened because you decided not to touch food that was right under your bondage.' When the lion asked what he meant, the crow quietly whispered in his ear: 'Chitrakarna'.

The lion immediately touched the ground with his hand and then raised it to his ears in a gesture of regret. 'I assured him he'd never have to fear for his life. How can I do this now? It has also been said:

> Of all the possible gifts
> one can make in this world,
> the gift of a fearless life is the greatest.
> Not so the gift of land, gold, cows, or grain. (56)

> Protecting a refugee
> even gives the same spiritual merit
> as performing the royal Ashvamedha sacrifice.' (57)

The crow then spoke: 'Certainly Your Highness should not kill him. But let the three of us get him to voluntarily offer the gift of his body!' The lion was silent on hearing this. Seizing his chance, the crow gathered everyone else and addressed the king publicly this time: 'Master, despite all our efforts, we could find no food for days on end. Your energy too is flagging. Here, please feed off my flesh. Because:

> The king is the true basis of all existence.
> Only if the roots survive, can the tree.' (58)

The lion, however, said: 'It is better to give up one's life than to indulge in such an act.' The tiger then stepped up and proposed his flesh for the king. The lion again refused, calling it inappropriate. Seeing this, in all innocence believing the others, poor Chitrakarna too offered his life, at which the tiger instantly ripped apart his belly, killing him. They all then partook of his flesh.

'And this is why I say that good people often get taken in and second-guess themselves by the words of the wicked,' said Meghavarna. 'So, when the third thug too accosted the Brahmin with the same words, the Brahmin concluded that he was imagining a dog to be a goat and, abandoning the animal right there, bathed and went home. The thugs then took away the goat and made a meal of him. And this is why I say that good people think everyone else is good too, and so are easily cheated by the wicked.'

The king then spoke: 'Meghavarna, how did you last so long amidst the enemies?'

Meghavarna replied: 'One has to go to all lengths to get Sire's work done. See:

> Do we not have to carry firewood on our heads
> in order to light a fire at home?

Does the river not wash the feet
of the very tree it uproots? (59)

As it has been said:

The clever person keeps the enemy close.
Like the old serpent killed off the frog.' (60)

On being queried by the king, Meghavarna began to narrate.

THE TWELFTH STORY

In an old garden there lived a serpent named Mandavisha (Slow Poison). He was too old to hunt for food and would just be found hanging near the pond. A frog asked him one day why he didn't go forage. The serpent despondently replied: 'Oh friend, why bother with one as unfortunate as me?' When the bemused frog insisted, the snake said: 'Friend, I once through bad luck bit the twenty-year-old talented son of a learned Brahmin Kaundinya of Brahmapura City. Seeing his beloved son dead, Kaundinya staggered and fell on the ground in shock. All his well-wishers from Brahmapura came and sat around him. As it has been said:

He who is by one's side
in festivals and funerals
in joy and in grief
in war and in famine
in rebellions and in the king's palace,
he alone is a true friend. (61)

An ascetic named Kapila spoke: 'Oh Kaundinya, you are foolish to be lamenting so. Listen:

As soon as one is born
transience attaches to the body

even before the mother's embrace.
So why lament death? (62)

Where have all the mighty kings
vanished in the passages of time
while the earth still stands witness
to their passing? (63)

The body is accompanied by its destruction.
Possessions are accompanied by problems.
Union is accompanied by separation.
Everything that has an origin has an end. (64)

The slow degradation of this mortal frame
is imperceptible till the very end.
Just like when water seeps out of an unbaked pot,
it is not perceptible till it is all gone. (65)

Like an executioner takes a condemned man
to the execution ground
step by step,
so does death approach the living
step by step,
closer and closer each day. (66)

Youth, beauty, life itself,
luxuries, wealth, and attachment
to kinfolk are all transient.
The intelligent person should remain detached
from these, therefore. (67)

Like two logs floating in the sea
sometimes come together
only to separate again,
so too do we meet and then separate from

our family and friends in this world. (68)

Relationships are as fleeting
as a traveller resting in the shade of a tree,
only to get up and resume his journey
sooner or later. (69)

In any case, this body
is made from the five elements.
Why bemoan then its return
to those elements? (70)

The more we cling to the joys of relationships,
the more it pains our heart. (71)

Our own body won't be with us for long.
Why hope for it from others then? (72)

Just as birth preordains death,
so too does union preordain separation. (73)

Attachments that appear joyous in the beginning
turn painful at the end.
Just like consuming delectable confectionery
that has spoilt. (74)

Just like the river flows and never returns,
so too days and nights pass
taking with them our years
never to return. (75)

The company of good people
brings great joys in this world.
But separation from them inevitably
yields grief as a pair. (76)

> This is why wise people
> do not seek company and attachments.
> For there is no cure for the pain
> that ensues from separation. (77)
>
> Great kings like Sagar and others
> performed deeds of piety and merit
> but then they too
> were lost to time. (78)
>
> Even the best of human strategies
> to counter death fail. (79)
>
> From the very moment of conception
> a person in fact begins to inch closer
> to his end. (80)

Therefore, please ponder this transient world. Grief is but the doing of ignorance. See:

> If death was the real cause of your grief,
> the grief would grow with time, not diminish.
> Hence it is ignorance that causes pain, not death. (81)

Therefore, steady yourself in this knowledge. Lament no further. Because:

> The only cure for grief
> is to not indulge it.' (82)

Listening to the monk, Kaundinya, as if awoken from deep sleep, spoke: 'There is no point to living in this hell-like home now. It is best I depart for the forest.'

But Kapila again said:

> 'Those with attachments are plagued by ills
> even in the forest.

While those who control their sense-attachments
perform penance even in their homes.
Those engaged in meritorious acts and detached from
passions make a penance grove of their homes. (83)

A grieving person, whatever stage of life he chooses,
should simply follow dharma, treating all living beings alike.
Shaving the head or adorning ochre robes—
such externals are not needed
for the pursuit of righteousness. (84)

Those who eat only to live,
fornicate only to bear children,
and speak only to utter the truth,
they sail through even hard times. (85)

As it has been said:

Oh Pandava! Bathe in the river of the soul
whose waters are the truth, good behaviour its banks,
self-control its fords,
and compassion its waves.
To bathe in mere water
does not cleanse the soul. (86)

In particular:

This world full of
birth and death, old age, disease, and sorrows
is best forsaken
by the man desirous of happiness. (87)

There is nothing but sorrow in this illusory world,
no real joy.
Only the cessation of one's sorrows
is known as joy.' (88)

Kaundinya then said: 'That is indeed how it is,' and then proceeded to curse me thus: 'From this day on, may you be but a vehicle for frogs!'

Kapila replied: 'You are still drowning in grief, you are in no position to listen to advice. Nonetheless, pay heed:

Company of people should be abjured
but if you can't, then keep the company of the virtuous.
For that alone heals. (89)

And, desires should be abjured
but if you can't, then indulge them only with your wife
for that alone heals.' (90)

'When Kapila's nectar-like advice had quelled the fire of Kaundinya's grief, the latter took to the life of an ascetic. And so, thanks to his curse, I am sitting here waiting to carry frogs on my back,' said the snake.

That frog then went and told the king of frogs, Jalapada (Water Bound) by name, about this episode. Jalapada then came and ascended the serpent's back and was carried about by him. By the very next day, however, the serpent could no longer roam much and crawled about slowly, at which the king of frogs queried why.

The serpent told him he was starving and had no energy. The king then told him that by his permission, he was free to eat the frogs! The serpent humbly accepted this beneficence and began to consume frogs, one by one. And then, when the pond had not a single frog left, he turned on the king frog and gobbled him up as well.

'And that is why I say the clever person keeps the enemy close,' said Meghavarna, and then proceeded to conclude 'Master, let the full account be, suffice it for me to say that Hiranyagarbha is the right person to sign a treaty with, so do go ahead.'

But the king said: 'What kind of opinion is that? We have defeated this king in battle. Now either he should stay in my servitude or we go to war again.'

At that moment, the parrot returned from Jambudvipa and announced: 'Oh master, the king of Sinhala Island has surrounded Jambudvipa!' Chitravarna exclaimed in disbelief and so the parrot repeated the stunning news. The vulture, however, in his heart of hearts marvelled at the strategic wisdom of Sarvagya, the Brahminy duck, minister of Hiranyagarbha.

The king meanwhile thundered: 'Forget this Hiranyagarbha, I will now go destroy the Sinhala king.'

Dooradarshi, the vulture, smiled and said:

'One shouldn't thunder in vain
like clouds in autumn.
Great men don't announce
what will become of their enemies.
They just act. (91)

And, further, a king must not fight
multiple enemies at once.
For many small ants
can bring down a mighty serpent. (92)

So, oh king, must you go without first concluding the treaty with Hiranyagarbha? If you do, you will face his rebellion as soon as you leave. And further:

The fool who gets enraged
without first grasping the truth,
suffers the same plight as the Brahmin
who repented over the mongoose.' (93)

When the king asked how that happened, Dooradarshi began to narrate.

THE THIRTEENTH STORY

There lived in the city of Ujjaini, a Brahmin by the name Madhava. His wife bore a child and, leaving Madhava to guard the newborn, she went off to bathe. At that same time, however, the Brahmin received a missive to come perform shraadh rituals for the king. Now, being poor of means, the Brahmin did not want to lose out on the opportunity. Because:

> In things worth doing
> and in matters of give and take,
> the whole point is lost
> if we delay. (94)

But there was nobody to entrust the baby to at home, so the Brahmin wondered what to do. At long last he decided that he would leave his pet mongoose to stand guard over the baby. Doing so, he left for the palace.

As it happened, a snake approached the child. The mongoose, however, instantly killed and tore it to pieces. When the Brahmin got home, the mongoose, covered in blood as he was, went and lay at the feet of the Brahmin. The Brahmin, however, jumped to the conclusion that it had devoured his baby and beat to death the poor mongoose.

It was only later when he saw his baby safely asleep and the dead snake nearby that he realized the huge mistake he had made. Seeing the loyal mongoose now lying dead, the Brahmin grieved in remorse.

'And this is why I say that the fool who acts before grasping the truth suffers grief and remorse,' concluded the vulture. And further:

'Desire, anger, attachment, greed,
arrogance, and intoxication—
these six vices are best abandoned.
In forsaking them a king prospers.' (95)

The king asked: 'Minister, is this your final decision?' So the vulture replied: 'Yes, it is. Because:

It is a minister's job
to be well-versed in dharma,
to be intelligent, stable of mind, determined,
and discreet in strategies. (96)

In any case:

One must never act in haste
for a lack of discriminating intellect
is the root of many a misfortune.
Whereas all good things come on their own
to one who applies his intellect before he acts. (97)

So, oh king, if you be pleased to listen to me, make peace with Hiranyagarbha before you set out against the Sinhala king. Because:

Even though four strategies of victory have been given,
namely, appeasement, bribe, coercion, and
creating discord among the enemy,
victory is best achieved through means of peace.' (98)

Doubtful, the king asked how this was possible, so the minister replied: 'Oh king, it will happen soon enough. See:

A fool is won over to peace easily
and a man of intelligence
even more easily.

> It is only a haughty man with little knowledge
> who holds out even against the gods. (99)

And it is well established from both Meghavarna's testimony and their actions that Hiranyagarbha and his minister Sarvagya are wise and righteous. Because:

> A person and his virtues
> must be judged by his actions
> if he's not around himself.
> And his intentions can be gauged
> from the end results.' (100)

'All right, enough of this discussion. Do what needs to be done,' said the king. So, the vulture said he would do what is best and entered the fortress.

Meanwhile, Hiranyagarbha's spy, the stork, informed him in advance that the minister vulture was coming to make peace. Hiranyagarbha, however, was suspicious and said as much to his minister, the Brahminy duck. The duck laughed and said: 'Oh king, now is not the time to be suspicious. Dooradarshi is a good man. And in any case, it is only people of low intellect who sometimes have no doubts at all and at other times, doubt everything and everyone.

> Once bitten, twice shy.
> A person once cheated in this world
> begins to doubt even the good.
> Like the swan who mistakes the reflection of stars in the
> pond for lotus stalks
> and so abjures the white lotus stalk even during the day,
> suspecting them to be the reflection of stars again. (101)

> People deceived by the wicked
> cease to trust even the good.
> Like a child burnt by porridge
> blows at even yoghurt to cool it down. (102)

Therefore, oh king, prepare to issue a grand welcome to Dooradarshi.'

Then the duck himself went to the entrance of the fortress and warmly received the vulture and ushered him in to Hiranyagarbha's presence. He was courteously seated there.

Then the duck addressed him saying: 'Everyone is subject to you here. You are free to rule this kingdom as you wish.' The king endorsed this. However, Dooradarshi said:

'Yes, it is indeed so. However, this is no time for formal speeches. Because:

> While the greedy may be won over by wealth,
> and the arrogant by hands folded in placation,
> the fool may be given what he wants,
> but the wise man may be won over
> by simply uttering the truth. (103)

> And further, it has been said:
> A friend should be persuaded with humility,
> relatives by sweet words,
> women by gifts and honour,
> so too servitors,
> and all the rest by cleverness. (104)

So kindly now come and sue for peace, King Chitravarna is great.'

'Do say how you want to sue for peace,' said the duck. Hiranyagarbha asked: 'How many kinds of peace are there?'

The vulture replied: 'I will explain, please listen.

One who has taken on a stronger enemy
and has no recourse but to sue for peace
in such a crisis
should approach and appeal to the king for the same. (105)

There are said to be sixteen kinds of peace treaties or alliances:
that which is on equal terms,
that in which one side gives gifts to the other,
that in which a daughter is gifted as a prelude,
and that which is founded on friendship.
This one is the Golden Treaty which lasts a lifetime
because the interests of both sides are represented. (106–12)

Then there is the alliance calculated to achieve only one's ends,
then that which is founded on obligation,
that which is based on expectation of reciprocation like
the one between Lord Rama and Sugriva,
that which has a common object and is secured firmly by proofs,
that in which a piece of land is ceded to a powerful enemy,
that in which interests are to be secured by armed forces or by particular third parties,
that in which everything is relinquished to the enemy in return for one's life,
that in which peace is made along with one's army,
that in which peace is made in return for a part of the treasury,
that in which very valuable lands are ceded,
and that in which the entire tax yielded by a land
is given away or that in which a part thereof is offered.
(113–23)

Of these, the alliances where there is reciprocal obligation,
friendship, marriage, and gifts exchanged
are the real peace treaties. (124)

And of these only the treaty based on gifts
is acceptable to me.
All others are bereft of friendship. (125)

A warrior returns with something or the other when he
lays siege.
So, there can be no treaty without gifts.' (126)

Then the duck said: 'Look:

This person is my own and that person a stranger—
this is the thinking
of the small-hearted.
For the magnanimous,
the whole world is family. (127)

Such a person is wise who regards
another's wife as his mother
another's wealth as mud
and all creatures as his own self.' (128)

The king then said: 'You people are learned and wise. Tell me what we need to do and we will do it.'

'Oh no, why do you say that?' the minister asked.

'Who will act unrighteously
for the sake of this body
which is here today and gone tomorrow,
afflicted by many ills? (129)

Life is as ephemeral
as the flickering reflection

of the moon in water.
Knowing this, one should always act
for good. (130)

The world is illusory like a mirage.
Hence, we must make truce with good people
for dharma and happiness. (131)

So, I think that's just what you should do. Because:

If you weigh a thousand royal sacrifices
against the truth,
it is truth that will weigh more by far.' (132)

So, in the interest of truth, I think these two kings should undertake the Golden Treaty.'

Sarvagya, the Brahminy duck, agreed. So, the royal swan, King Hiranyagarbha, then feted Dooradarshi with many gifts and saw him off. The latter along with the duck left for the court of the peacock king Chitravarna where, on the advice of the vulture, the king respectfully addressed the Brahminy duck and accepted the Golden Treaty.

After the duck was seen off, Dooradarshi said: 'Oh king, we have achieved what we sought. Now we should return to our home, the Vindhyas.' This they all promptly did and lived happily after.

◆

At this point Vishnusharma paused and then said: 'What else should I narrate? Tell me.' The princes replied: 'Thanks to your grace, we have learnt the art of politics. It is already more than we could ask for and we are delighted.'

'If that's so,' said Vishnusharma, 'then may this too happen:

> May triumphant kings always be pleased by their alliances,
> may good people always be free of troubles,
> may the doers of virtuous deeds enjoy fame for aeons,
> and may the science of prudent conduct
> always reside in the hearts of ministers.' (133)

And, further:

> May this collection of stories by Pandit Narayana
> circulate and be famous
> till as long as the crescent-bearing Shiva,
> and the daughter of the Himalaya, Parvati,
> are together.
> And till as long as Lakshmi resides in the heart of Vishnu,
> like brilliant lightning among dark clouds.
> And till as long as Meru, the golden mountain
> with the sun its sparking summit,
> stands unmoving in its place. (134)

> And, may the illustrious ruler Dhavalachandra,
> who caused this collection of stories
> to be composed and promoted,
> forever triumph over all his enemies. (135)

And here ends the *Hitopadesha*.

ACKNOWLEDGEMENTS

The people I would like to thank for this book could easily belong in it! All the dogs I have known, and with whom I have had the privilege of sharing my life, ever since I was nine years old. They have done for me what animals do best: make one feel alive.

My gratitude also to my husband, Nachiketa, for always supporting my work with street and rescue dogs, and my sister, Devika, for her love of nature.